Iridescent Feathers

July 12, 2015

Robert Marcin

Robert Marcin

dedicated to:

Finding a Cure for Alzheimer's

iii

CONTENTS

A   Fictional Yarn — Inspired by True Events

PROLOGUE: MYSTICAL LIGHT

On the Sunday after Thanksgiving, Jimmy ate the usual leftovers; watched football on TV; practiced a few guitar rifts; and went to bed. He was sleeping soundly when he curiously began to glow with the same mystical light that had, twice before, brought him back to life. His eyes suddenly opened and he got out of bed in a trance-like state. He went straight to his desk, apparently in search of something, and quickly removed a reporter's notebook and a pencil from the top left drawer. He placed the notebook on top of the desk, remained standing, and began to write. After he finished writing, he put the pencil on top of the notebook and went back to bed. He pulled his blanket up over his body, placed his head on his pillow, and closed his eyes. The mystical light vanished, and he was, once again, fast-asleep. A white iridescent fluffy down feather perched, mysteriously, on the notebook.

CHAPTER 1:   THE FIRST FEATHER

James Marshall Masden was unintentionally conceived, on a pleasant autumn evening, at a campground in the general vicinity of Camp David and Mount Saint Mary's replica of the Grotto of Lourdes in Frederick County, Maryland. He was due to be born on the Fourth of July. His parents, Joe and Lynn Masden, were elated—because they were married on the Fourth of July.

His mother had given birth to Jenny and Jack, his two older siblings, without a hitch—but, that would not be the case with Jimmy. For some unknown reason, Lynn's water started leaking in mid-February and she was given the options to end the pregnancy or go to bed until she gave birth. She wisely chose the latter.

Early in the evening, on the 10th of May, Lynn walked out of the bathroom and instantly dropped to the floor. She was bleeding and in pain. Joe instinctively dialed 911. The dead preemie began glowing with a mystical light. His heart started beating, and the mystical light vanished. The ambulance arrived quickly; and when it arrived at its destination—the entrance to the emergency room of Frederick Memorial Hospital—the doctor on duty immediately entered the ambulance, cut Lynn's vagina, and pulled Jimmy out. The delivery was breach. By the time Joe arrived, the

doctor was busy stitching Lynn in the blood-
spattered ambulance, and Jimmy's pediatrician was
manually pumping air into his tiny lungs in the
emergency room. Joe naturally peeked inside the
ambulance and curiously noticed a white iridescent
fluffy down feather perched, beside his wife, on
the floor of the ambulance.

Weighing a little over three pounds, Jimmy
was given an Apgar score of zero and almost no
chance to survive. He was transported by ambulance
to Saint Agnes Hospital in Baltimore, Maryland,
and admitted into their neo-natal intensive care
unit—where he remained for nearly one month. His
parents anxiously managed to visit him everyday.
Lynn kept them supplied with breast-milk, which
the nurses called "liquid gold," to keep him
nourished with the much-needed vitamins, minerals,
and antigens that he needed to survive. He was
transferred back to Frederick Memorial Hospital,
in the middle of June, and subsequently released
into his parents' care on the Fourth of July—his
initial due date, and his parents' 13th wedding
anniversary.

Jimmy was a textbook baby—who sufficiently
mastered everything in the widely accepted pre-
determined order. He also grew to become very
strong for his age, and he was blessed with
exceptional balance and speed. Joe sincerely

believed that his youngest son might have a future in sports.

CHAPTER 2:   GROWING-UP MASDEN

After Jimmy was born, Joe and Lynn took
their children to visit with their respective
families, in New York and Virginia, almost every
summer and occasionally in conjunction with the
winter and spring holidays. They usually went to
New York for a few days around the Fourth of July.
While they were there, they visited many of the
tourist attractions in New York City.

When Jimmy was two years old, they went to
the 102nd floor observation deck of the Empire
State Building. Jenny and Jack were "on top of the
world" and thoroughly enjoying themselves; but,
Jimmy let out a fearful scream when Joe picked him
up to show him the amazing view. It took Lynn
quite a while to calm him down, before they could
take the elevator ride back down to the ground
floor.

They visited the Statue of Liberty and Ellis
Island several times over the years. Jimmy
especially loved Lady Liberty and the ferry ride.
When Jimmy was six years old, they took the ferry
to Ellis Island to locate Joe's grandparents'
names on the American Immigrant Wall of Honor. His
paternal grandparents emigrated from
Czechoslovakia and his maternal grandparents were
both Italian immigrants. When they arrived, Joe
successfully searched for their names on a

computer that gave the locations of all the names
currently on the Wall of Honor—after which, they
immediately proceeded outside and quickly found
the exquisite engravings. Joe took pictures, and
diligently used a pencil and a piece of paper to
make a rubbing of each name. Once that pleasant
task was completed, they were taking a few moments
to admire the entire Wall of Honor and relish in
the plethora of sights that surrounded them—when
Jimmy suddenly ran to the edge of the island that
faced the Statue of Liberty and yelled at the top
of his lungs, "We found them! We found them!"
There were several signs posted in the area asking
everyone to observe a respectful silence, and Lynn
panicked. She rushed to Jimmy and asked, "Why are
you screaming so loud?" He very excitedly said,
"Because, she has to know!" Lynn asked, "Who are
you talking to?" He enthusiastically replied, "The
Lady—Lady Liberty needs to know that we found the
names!" There was an elderly couple standing
nearby, so Lynn took Jimmy by the hand and
approached them to apologize for his outburst.
They had tears in their eyes. After Lynn
apologized, they gave each other a hug and turned
their attention to Jimmy. The elderly woman said,
"I am quite pleased with your decision to tell
Lady Liberty that you found the names you were
searching for, and I truly believe that it made
her very happy."

Several Fourth of July's were spent watching the Yankees take on the Orioles in the "old" Yankee Stadium. Joe's father always managed to get them prime seats, and all three children dearly loved the experience. On each occasion, Joe's mother had their Fourth of July wedding anniversary announced, in the form of emblazoned congratulations, on the centerfield screen—a very special something that their children will surely never forget.

Believe it or not, one of Jimmy's "favorite things" was the drive home from New York to Maryland. He could not wait to view the New York City skyline as they crossed the George Washington Bridge and continued traveling south on the New Jersey Turnpike to Pennsylvania. He was absolutely devastated when the infamous tragedy of 9/11 took the twin towers of the World Trade Center out of the picture, and he sincerely grieved for the senseless loss of human life and excruciating pain the families of lost loved ones were unforgivably forced to endure.

Woodsville Middle School traditionally took their 8th grade class on a field trip to the World Trade Center. Jenny and Jack went on that field trip when they were in the 8th grade, but Jimmy would never get the chance, because he was in the 2nd grade on 9/11. In the summer of 2002, Joe and Lynn took him to witness the aftermath. It

undoubtedly left an indelible memory, of an
incredible tragedy, forever etched in his young
mind.

The family's annual visits with Lynn's
family, in Rockbridge County, Virginia, gave their
children the opportunity to experience a very
different perspective of life in America. Lynn is
a descendent of very early German and English
settlers, and she is a bona fide Daughter of the
American Revolution. There was Grammy, Pa Taylor,
Pa Keltz, Loretta, Grandma, Grandpa, and hundreds
of acres of well-maintained farmland remotely
nestled amidst tranquil mountains.

Grammy, Pa Taylor, and Loretta are gone now;
but a spry, 99 years young, Pa Keltz was still
running around, and each of them respectfully
cherished every waning chance they had to visit
with him. Their children loved them. They had a
great time pretending to make apple butter at
Grammy's, catching fish in Pa Keltz's pond, taking
tractor rides with Grandpa, and eating Grandma's
time-honored, traditional down-home cooking.

Rockbridge County, Virginia may arguably
showcase some of the most breathtaking mountain
views in the country, that notwithstanding, their
family that lives there are certainly among the
most wonderful human beings with which their
children were very fortunate to have had the

opportunity to enjoy some incomparable quality-time. They will never forget the peaceful serenity and love that they felt, on the family farm, in Buena Vista, Virginia.

CHAPTER 3:   HIGH SCHOOL CHALLENGES

Following in his older brother's footsteps,
Jimmy was an athletic "stud," throughout his
youth, in both baseball and football.
Unfortunately, his freshmen high school year
became the beginning of his end. The people he
chose to hang out with had a very negative
attitude towards school and smoked marijuana. In
the beginning, he started smoking marijuana and
misbehaving in school mostly just to appease them—
but, shortly thereafter, he became addicted.

His sophomore football season mysteriously
began with a badly broken leg. The varsity team
was scrimmaging the junior varsity team, in the
traditional pre-season Blue-White game, when Jimmy
was injured. Joe had just left the house to go to
the post office when the phone rang. Lynn answered
the phone, "Hello." The caller asked, "Is this
Mrs. Masden?" She replied, "Yes." He responded,
"This is coach Kerry. Jimmy's been injured and I
need you to come to the football field." She
immediately rushed to the high school; and, when
she arrived, coach Kerry greeted her saying, "It
looks like Jimmy may have broken a bone in his
right leg."

Joe surprisingly returned to an empty house,
and nervously called Lynn's cell phone. She
quickly answered, "I'm at the high school football

field because Jimmy may have a broken leg, and he is going to be transported by ambulance to Frederick Memorial Hospital. I will ride in the ambulance. Please, meet me there." Joe arrived at the hospital shortly before his son went into surgery. Jimmy's right femur was severely fractured, just above the knee along its growth plate, and he had to have three screws put in it—to aid in the healing process. He was also, very unfortunately, introduced to prescribed narcotic pain-killers.

It was, in the very least, a season-ending injury for Jimmy—and, in some ways, he appeared to be relieved. He had previously told several relatives and friends—in the off-season between his freshmen and sophomore years—that he did not want to play football. However, it was difficult for Joe and Lynn to get a handle on what he was truly feeling. Considering his age, and the fact that he was never adamant when he spoke to either of them on the topic of playing high school football, clearly indicated to them that it might have just been talk.

On the other hand, his latest circle of friends were into the 70's, Rock and Roll, and all of the drugs associated with that era. He lied to his parents saying, "Some of my friends' parents were hippies back in the 70's and have not changed their ways; but, I can honestly assure you that I am not doing anything wrong or illegal." He was taking his parents for fools. Nevertheless, even in hindsight, Joe was not sure if the narcotics Jimmy had taken for pain, when he broke his leg, were responsible for initiating his probable indulgence, or if they just added to it. Jenny and Jack were fully aware of what their younger brother was doing. Joe told Lynn, on many occasions, "Jimmy is smoking marijuana and stealing my cigarettes." Lynn did not want to believe it, and she somehow managed to convince herself that it was not happening.

Shortly after he was declared healed, Jimmy began spending progressively increasing amounts of his free time at a development located a few miles north of his, Slade Acres, that he simply referred to as Slade. Lynn sincerely believed that his "new" circle of friends could potentially be beneficial—because some of them were athletes on the high school football team, and she was hoping that they might talk him into playing again. Joe tried to be just as optimistic, but he had some legitimate lingering doubts. He sincerely believed that his son was much more interested in marijuana and pain-killers.

When Jimmy's sophomore year entered the spring—his behavior, attitude, and grades began cascading in a downward spiral. He was still spending some time with his friends in Pinewood, his development—which had a notorious reputation as an easy place to find gangs and drugs—until his closest friend moved. After his friend moved, he began spending most of his free time in Slade, and his general attitude toward just about everything quickly deteriorated.

Jimmy began flirting with becoming incorrigible. By the time the fourth school term arrived, he was skipping his last class and refusing to do any schoolwork in each of his classes. He was eventually caught for skipping his last class, and he was suspended from school. It was somewhat difficult for Joe to imagine that, because his son wrongfully chose to skip one of his classes, he was now legally skipping all of them. Nevertheless, because of his noncompliance, Jimmy miserably failed all of his fourth-term courses.

CHAPTER 4: THE SUMMER

The Masdens usually found time, each summer, to visit with their families in Westchester County, New York and Rockbridge County, Virginia. Fortunately, this summer was no exception.

Their first excursion was on the 30th of June. They took Jimmy to Virginia to celebrate the 50th wedding anniversary of Lynn's parents. Jimmy met several relatives and family friends, for the first time, and he left a lasting good impression. He awed everyone with his natural charisma, close resemblance to Nick Jonas, and Eddie Haskell manners. Joe was disappointedly surprised by his son's demeanor, and the way he slyly misrepresented the current edition of himself.

The celebration was held in the recreation center of the Methodist church, where Lynn's parents had worshipped their Lord for almost their entire lives. It was a simple, well-planned observance of a milestone achievement that was amicably received, and the Masdens endearingly enjoyed having the opportunity to socialize with relatives and family friends that they had not seen for many years. Joe and Lynn had tears in their eyes, and very warm hearts, when they expeditiously left the following morning—to return home and celebrate their wedding anniversary on the Fourth of July.

It was very reminiscent of the Fourth of July celebrations they had when Jenny and Jack were toddlers. They spent the day at Frederick's annual commemoration in Baker Park, and the early evening taking in the sights and sounds of Woodsville's annual carnival. They decided to replace the carnival's fireworks with Macy's televised version, and spent the night blissfully cuddled in each other's arms.

They had planned on going to New York to visit Joe's family, on July 5th, with strong hopes of letting Jack stay there with his grandfather and continue commuting to college. Joe believed that it would be advantageous for Jack, who was going to be a sophomore, to start conditioning for his football camp that was scheduled to start in the first week of August. Jack anxiously agreed with his father.

Before they left for New York, Joe and Lynn made plans to go to a beach on Long Island. However, at the last minute, Jimmy unexpectedly pleaded with them to change their plans and go to New York City. Initially, Joe firmly refused. Then, he took some time to brainstorm a favorable alternative with Lynn, and he reluctantly agreed to do something that he believed would appease his youngest son. Joe knew that Jimmy was a John Lennon fan—so, he reasoned that he might enjoy seeing the building John Lennon and Yoko Ono had

lived in, the Dakota, and Strawberry Fields—
conveniently located a short distance away in
Central Park.

Perhaps fatefully, on July 6th, they took the
train to Grand Central Station and decided to walk
to the Dakota. It was a perfect day—low humidity,
highs in the low 80's, and not a cloud in the sky.
After lunch, at a Central Park eatery, they made
their way to the Dakota and admired its
architectural beauty. They walked all the way
around the legendary building, and then sat on a
bench across the street—where the three of them
tried, in vain, to discern the location of John
Lennon's apartment.

Shortly thereafter, they found themselves
sitting on one of the benches in Strawberry
Fields. Some of the strangers were playing
guitars, and a very weird man was trying to sell
John Lennon memorabilia while eerily talking to
himself at the same time. A wide-eyed Jimmy took
all of it in, as he was quietly having the time of
his life. A group of young school-aged children,
apparently on a field trip, passed through. All of
the benches were fully occupied by people relaxing
on a gorgeous day in the park. The one thing
everyone seemed to have in common was the
admiration of a tiled mosaic, in the center of the
walkway, entitled "Imagine."

After they left Strawberry Fields, they quickly strolled through the park toward the southeast exit. When they arrived at the exit, just outside of the world renowned Plaza Hotel, Jimmy started looking at all the framed photographs of the "Imagine" mosaic that were being sold by almost every vendor. He quickly purchased one, and they immediately started making their way back to Grand Central Station. They were slowly walking where the multitude of tour guides were pitching their horse-and-carriage rides when Joe stopped and asked, "Jimmy, would you like to take a horse-and-carriage ride through Central Park?" Less than a minute later, they were boarding one for a ride through the section of Central Park where some of Home Alone 2 was filmed. They thoroughly enjoyed the experience and unanimously agreed to do it again. Then, they started walking, for the second time, in the direction of Grand Central Station.

They were casually walking south on 5th Avenue when a significantly large number of police cars, with lights on and sirens blasting, speeded passed them traveling in the same direction. They quickened their pace, and anxiously boarded the commuter train back to Tuckahoe. When they arrived at Joe's father's condo, he informed them that the police in New York City had successfully aborted a potentially serious terrorist threat.

They spent the evening visiting with relatives, window-shopping at a nearby outdoor mall, and ended the night sharing stories with Joe's father. In the early morning hours of the following day, they packed their bags and drove back to their home in Maryland.

When they were in New York, Jimmy started talking about getting the three screws in his right leg removed. He begged his mom stating, "As long as I have the screws in my leg, I will have to take an antibiotic every time I go to the dentist, and I could never have a full-body MRI. I will also set-off every security device in the world that is testing for the presence of anything metal." Lynn compassionately agreed, but she was intuitively concerned with his mention of the MRI dilemma. So, she called the orthopedic surgeon, who had put the screws in, and made an ASAP appointment to have them removed.

On July 15th, Jimmy had the surgical steel screws removed. The successful procedure did not take very long, and he seemed to be happy that they were gone, but the resultant pain told him otherwise. After he broke his leg, he was introduced to the world of addictive painkillers, and the removal of the screws enigmatically culminated with his second introduction. Unfortunately, he experienced a serious allergic reaction to the prescribed pain medication and

Lynn had to rush, on an emergency basis, to procure an antidotal prescription. Fortunately, his doctor ordered another painkiller that agreed with him.

Jimmy and his father finally settled into a summer-time routine. The surgery to remove the screws in his leg was a relatively minor procedure, and despite the fact that he had three small holes in his right femur, he was quickly quite mobile. Less than two weeks later, he was very capably walking without crutches and riding his bike.

On a typical summer day, Joe arose with Lynn, drank a few cups of home-brewed Starbuck's coffee, and saw her off to work. Shortly after she left—Joe took a shower, got dressed, put the dirty clothes in the washer, and got busy working on a summer project. He stopped working at around 11:00 AM to answer a phone call from Lynn, after which, he folded the clothes that he had washed and dried, and prepared lunch. Jimmy would be awake in his room watching television—patiently waiting for his dad to inform him that lunch was ready. After they ate lunch together—Jimmy walked, rode his bike, or asked his dad to drop him off at Slade. After which, Joe went to the community pool to relax in the sun and get some exercise. If he drove Jimmy to Slade that day, which was usually the case, he picked him up at around 4:30 PM. After they got home, Joe started making dinner.

In reality, things were a bit more topsy-turvy than they appeared to be. "Who" was on first; "What" was on second; and "I Don't Know" was on third—but, at the time, Joe felt at least as frustrated as Lou Costello was when Bud Abbott subjected him to that timeless scenario. Jimmy was not his usual self. There was something very different about him.

CHAPTER 5: "THE SECOND FEATHER"

The relatively catastrophic events, from a family perspective, which occurred on Thursday, August 24, changed the Masdens' lives forever. The day began just like each of the past three days; Joe and Lynn went to work and 16-year-old Jimmy was left to fend for himself. When Joe went back to work, on August 23rd, Jimmy lost his daily commute to Slade. It really did not faze him, because he could either walk or ride his bike. He usually chose to ride his bike, because it was faster than walking. He would leave his bike at a friend's house in Slade and they would walk to their chosen destination. Afterwards, he would return to his friend's house to retrieve his bike, and ride it back home to have dinner. After dinner, he would ask his dad to drive him back to Slade and pick him up later. However, for a reason known only to him, for the past three days—he chose to ride his bike. Lynn was not too worried about him riding it during the day, but she was very concerned about his decision to ride it on busy roads after dark. She was intrinsically wary about motorists being able to see him, and she very clearly expressed her feelings on a regular basis. Jimmy would play the role of a typical 16-year-old and act as if he was just ignoring her. This day, the unusual would be the norm. Jimmy did not ignore his mother's caring concern; he chose to reply instead. Lynn was trying her best to, yet again, warn him about the difficulty motorists would have seeing him riding his bike in the dark. Jimmy paused, quickly turned to face her, and abruptly said, "It has reflectors on it." Then, he pulled a battery-operated lighted key chain out of his pocket, and sarcastically said, "I could use this to make myself more visible." Lynn attempted to reason with him saying, "That light could easily be mistaken for a firefly. Please, let your father drive you." He laughingly put the key chain back into his pocket and quickly replied, "I'll be home around ten, if I don't get hit by a car." Then, he immediately left through the back door, got on his bike, and rode it to Slade.

Jimmy easily made it to Dave's—his squirrely-looking friend's house. After which, they left on foot to go to another friend's house. In order to get to their mutual friend's house, they had to cross Route 176. Maryland Route 176 is a two-lane highway that runs north and south between its intersection with Maryland Route 48 in Frederick, Maryland and the Pennsylvania border. Route 176, including the Woodsville bypass, is clearly posted with a rather unreasonable 50 mph speed limit. There is a traffic light and crosswalk at the end of the Woodsville bypass; and a second traffic light, and crosswalk, a short

distance north of it. Both crosswalks were fairly
well equipped with pedestrian stop and go signals,
and adequate street lights.

At approximately 8:35 PM, Jimmy and Dave
started walking back to Dave's house. Jimmy was
going to get his bike and ride it back home. A
black four wheel drive Chevy Blazer was heading
north on Route 176, through the Woodsville bypass,
at exactly the same time. Jimmy and Dave decided
to cross Route 176 between the two crosswalks,
because the shortest distance between two points
is a straight line and they both enjoyed having
the invincible mentality of typical 16-year-olds.
When they arrived at their poorly chosen crossing
point, they immediately began to jog across—
because, "cars have brakes."

Dave saw the black Chevy Blazer approaching
and stopped. Jimmy apparently did not see what he
was running into and kept going. The Chevy Blazer
went through a green light, cruising at the 50 mph
posted speed limit. Very shortly thereafter, the
driver barely caught a glimpse of Jimmy running in
front of him in the dusky dark. He slammed on
the brakes and struck a basically stationary Jimmy
traveling over 40 mph. The front bumper hit
Jimmy's right leg where the three recently removed
screws left three not-yet-healed holes in his
right femur. The driver-side hood fiercely drove
his right arm into his liver, ribs, and right

lung. The hood buckled and the air bags deployed. Jimmy's helpless body was simultaneously lifted on top of the buckled hood, and the right side of his head bounced off the passenger-side windshield. In the stillness of the night, the ferocious sound of the collision was easily heard more than a mile away. The incredible force of the impact violently tossed him to the road, where he hit the left side of his head and slid on the pavement—inflicting a significant amount of "road-rash" to his face, upper torso, arms, legs, and feet. His shoes were, upon impact, ejected and propelled over 90 feet away into an empty lot. The incomprehensible severity of the extremely unbalanced force quickly, and kindly, took his life. Jimmy's lifeless body, slowly dripping blood from a deep gash in his left eyebrow, harshly came to rest on the shoulder of Route 176.

The young man, who was driving the Chevy Blazer, instinctively dialed 911 on his cell phone. They quickly answered, and he nervously replied, "My name is Adam Grove. I'm a state policeman, and I just struck a young pedestrian with my SUV. Send a bus, ASAP, to the intersection of Route 176 and Bluestone Drive in Woodsville." The 911 operator immediately dispatched a Woodsville ambulance and contacted the Maryland State Police Medevac Unit for a potential transfer.

A very large crowd of curious on-lookers, who were startled by the intense sound of the impact, began to gather. A mother and son that Joe and Lynn had known for many years, and lived nearby, were fortunately among the on-lookers who had rushed to the scene of the accident. The worried mother and her son, Tony, were running across the road towards Jimmy's lifeless body, when he suddenly began to glow with an apparent heaven-sent light. They stopped dead in their tracks. Then, they surprisingly witnessed him gasping for air and begin breathing. The ambient glow mysteriously disappeared as they cautiously approached him. The caring mother sent her son to inform Joe and Lynn, and compassionately stayed with Jimmy until the ambulance arrived. While she was waiting, she curiously noticed a white iridescent fluffy down feather perched, unscathed, on the pavement beside Jimmy's head.

The Woodsville Volunteer Fire Company sent almost everything they had to the scene. Two hook and ladder fire trucks effectively blocked the road in both directions, and one fully equipped ambulance transported EMTs to assess the injuries and attempt to stabilize him until the state police Medevac EMTs arrived. The state police Medevac EMTs were arriving on the scene as Tony was banging on the aluminum siding adjacent to Joe and Lynn's locked front storm door. His frantic

banging left dents in the siding that Joe would
curiously notice more than a month later. Joe
quickly opened the door. An adrenaline fueled Tony
immediately said, "Mr. and Mrs. Masden get
dressed! Jimmy was hit by an SUV near Stop and
Shop! My mother's with him, and you know she's
almost a nurse. She said to tell you that he was
breathing. He's breathing, hurry-up!" They quickly
changed clothes, as best they could, and rushed
out of the house in a total state of panic and
shock. Tony politely asked, "Could you please take
me with you? I hitched a ride here." They, of
course, said "Yes."

When they arrived on the scene—Joe parked in
an open space he located in the middle of the
blocked road, and they all got out of the car. He
immediately observed the badly damaged four wheel
drive Chevy Blazer; hundreds of distant on-
lookers; the ambulance; and the running state
police Medevac helicopter. Shortly thereafter, he
heard someone say, "The man told the police that
he was traveling more than 40 mph when he hit the
boy." Joe and Lynn just stood there, perplexed and
bewildered, because there was nothing they could
do. Jimmy was out-of-sight, in an ambulance, being
prepped for a Medevac transfer. Joe, once again,
observed the external damage and deployed air bags
of the SUV that had struck his son, and fear
immediately accompanied the panic and shock that

was clearly visible in his eyes. Tony turned to him and said, "Don't worry coach, Jimmy's a Masden and Masdens are tough." Joe was an assistant varsity football coach, at Woodsville High School, when Tony played football there with Jack. Joe could only speculate that Tony was equating Jimmy's toughness with what he had experienced with Jack. Silently, Joe was sincerely hoping and praying that he was right.

The ambulance's back doors opened. An unconscious Jimmy, strapped to a gurney and intubated with nasotracheal oxygen tubes, was swiftly rushed to the running Medevac helicopter. His parents barely got a glimpse of him, and they were instantly overwhelmed with shock-driven anxiety. Joe instinctively wanted to know what they should do next. Without thinking, he quickly approached one of the Woodsville firefighters and asked, "Can you tell how my son is doing, and where he is being taken?" The fireman solemnly said, "I don't know his condition, but he is being transported to the R. Adams Cowley Shock Trauma Center in Baltimore." Joe politely asked, "Could you please give me directions?" The fireman quickly entered the ambulance and removed a sheet of paper from a three-ring binder, with directions on it, and quietly handed it to him. Joe said, "Thank you," and silently headed, with a teary-eyed Lynn, in the direction of their parked car.

CHAPTER 6:   SHOCK AND TRAUMA

Scared to death, Joe cautiously drove himself and his very worried wife home. After they arrived, Lynn quickly tried to compose herself and immediately phoned Jenny—to tell her what had happened and discuss their predicament. Emotionally, Joe was in no condition to drive to Baltimore. Even with directions, he had not driven there enough to be vaguely familiar with where he was supposed to be going. He also had an eye condition that made it very difficult for him to drive in the dark. Lynn had never driven to Baltimore. They were securely stuck between the rather obvious "rock and a hard place." Jenny explained their situation to her husband, Bill, and he unselfishly offered to drive them. Bill, a licensed contractor and carpenter, was very familiar with the area where they were taking Jimmy. Joe and Lynn agreed to that plan of action, changed clothes, and anxiously awaited their arrival. While they were waiting, they both contacted their respective employers to inform them of their present situation and request leave for an undetermined period of time. Their employers were very understanding and compassionately concurred. They mutually decided not to contact either of their families, in fear

of worrying them, until they could ascertain some
more reliable concrete information.

Bill and Jenny arrived about twenty minutes
later, and Lynn insisted that they take her car.
They switched cars, and Bill began driving to The
University of Maryland's Medical Center in
Baltimore. Joe read the directions aloud, from the
sheet that the Woodsville fireman gave him, and he
tried his best to observe the route. Jimmy's
helicopter ride took about twenty minutes, which
meant that they were leaving as he was arriving.
It took them a little over an hour to get there,
park in the underground parking garage, and walk
into the unfamiliar hospital—only to find out what
they should do next. Lynn explained their
situation to a woman manning the hospital's front
desk, and she instantly responded by issuing each
of them clip-on hospital passes and directing them
to the shock trauma center situated at the rear of
the main hospital.

They quickly located the shock trauma
center, and Lynn worriedly approached their
receptionist's desk to inquire about Jimmy. The
nice lady working at the desk immediately phoned
someone. She successfully spoke to someone,
somewhere, and tried to smile. Then, she hung the
phone up and said, "Your son is here, but they're
not quite ready for you. Please, have a seat in
the waiting area and I'll let you in to see him as

soon as I can." Bill, Jenny, and Joe briefly
complied. Lynn could not sit; she just paced back
and forth. Joe and Bill left to find a restroom,
while Jenny sat and Lynn paced. They returned
shortly, but Joe could not sit. He quickly walked
to the front entrance of the hospital, and exited
to smoke a cigarette. Lynn continued to pace,
until she was suddenly called up to the
receptionist's desk. She was hoping that the kind
lady was going to let her see her son, but she was
disappointedly asked for insurance information.
When Joe returned—Bill and Jenny were sitting in
the waiting area, and Lynn was still pacing. He
took a seat and noticed a "Why is it Taking so
Long?" message on the wall he was facing. He got
up slowly, and swiftly approached the wall to read
it. The message simply stated that it took time
to run tests and obtain the results.

Thursday became Friday at midnight.
Approximately one-half hour later, they were
allowed to see their critical-but-stable son in
shock trauma's emergency room—the TRU. At first
glance, Jimmy was unconscious and almost
unrecognizable. He was lying on his back in the
hospital bed that he would remain in as long as
he was a patient there. He was breathing, with the
assistance of a ventilator, and connected by wires
to a machine that monitored heart rate, blood
pressure, oxygen level, and body temperature. An

intravenous tube carrying water for hydration, and a simple sugar for energy, was properly inserted and functioning. An invasive tube had been inserted to transport liquid waste. The very bleak vision of her 16-year-old son's condition was more than Lynn could take and she began to feel queasy. Jimmy's nurse somehow recognized her symptoms and placed a chair at the foot of his hospital bed. Lynn thanked the nurse and sat down, but she was too concerned about her youngest child to remain there very long. Every couple of minutes, she would get up to be closer to him. Shortly thereafter, she started feeling queasy and returned to her seat. Still in shock, Joe quietly remained standing at the foot of the bed. It appeared to him that his son had been viciously beaten with a baseball bat and there was no way he was going to survive. He became concerned with Lynn's anxious up-and-down behavior and caringly suggested that they take a break to let Jenny and Bill see Jimmy. Lynn reluctantly agreed and shared their intentions with Jimmy's nurse. Sufficiently armed with the nurse's permission, they left the TRU. A teary-eyed Lynn told Jenny and Bill, "You could go back and see Jimmy. We need to get some fresh air." They walked straight to the hospital's front entrance and quickly exited. After which, they smoked their cigarettes and returned, without permission, directly to the TRU.

The TRU's rules very clearly stated that only two
visitors were allowed at a time, but Jimmy's nurse
compassionately let all four of them stay with
him.

Jimmy had been assigned to a team of six
world-renowned physicians, and his attending
physician was the doctor in charge of the shock
trauma center. At one point, Jimmy's nurse turned
to Lynn and said, "If anyone can save your son—
they can. They wrote the books." The handsome
attending physician, of Italian descent, finally
approached a nearly numb Joe and Lynn at around
2:00 AM. He introduced himself, and matter of
factly stated, "It's too early to know where we
stand. I'm sending him for a full body MRI that
will probably take most of the night." Lynn
thanked him and politely requested that he keep
her informed. Joe silently pondered the
significance of getting the surgical steel screws
removed from Jimmy's leg just a few weeks ago.

Jenny and Bill had to go home. They were
scheduled to close on a house they were buying,
later that same day, in Damascus, MD. They only
took one car, so either Joe or Lynn would have to
go back with them. They also left Zoso, the family
dog, unattended. Joe volunteered to ride back with
them, take care of Zoso, and return later in the
morning. So, they left Lynn in the TRU's waiting

room, rushed to the parking garage, and drove her Honda Civic back to Woodsville.

After they left, Lynn approached the receptionist's desk to inform her that she was going to stay. The receptionist said, "You should have gone home with your husband. Why would you want to stay here?" Lynn lovingly stated, "Because he's my son." The receptionist immediately left her post to get her a pillow and a blanket, and caringly ushered her into an enclosed waiting room that was clearly labeled "Quiet." Less than 10 minutes later, one of Jimmy's doctors walked into the waiting room and approached Lynn. She immediately thought the worst, but he calmly said, "Hello, everything's OK—I just need you to sign some papers authorizing permission to perform more tests."

After he left, Lynn's adrenaline rush prevented her from getting the rest she needed, so she got up and started pacing again. The back and forth pacing just made her anxiety level peak to a point of no return. She took a detour to the front entrance of the hospital and quickly exited to smoke a cigarette. While she was there, she was greeted by several strangers wanting to bum cigarettes. She told each of them that it was her last one, and decided that it would be in her best interest if she found a less-intrusive place to smoke.

Later on, she successfully managed to locate an outdoor smoking lounge where many doctors, nurses, and patients went to satisfy their addiction. She did not have to worry about indigents trying to bum cigarettes, but several curious hospital workers approached her to inquire about the circumstances that had landed her there. She took a deep breath and calmly shared her story with them. One of the female listeners, who just happened to be familiar with the situation, tried to assure her that the Medevac crew who transported her son was one of the best in the state. "Trooper 3," she said, "always brings detailed reports, and photos of the accident scene. The detailed reports, and photos, usually prove to be invaluable in the early treatment of critical injuries." This somewhat comforting information somehow relieved Lynn, so she returned to the waiting room—hoping to get some rest.

Meanwhile, Joe was en route, with Jenny and Bill, to his split-level rancher in Woodsville. Joe was exhausted. After they arrived, Joe appreciatively said, "Thank you very much. Have a good night and drive safely." Then, he swiftly entered his house and immediately tried to call Lynn on her cell phone. There was no answer. He rushed upstairs to their bedroom, quickly changed into his bedclothes, rushed back downstairs to the kitchen, and tried phoning her again. She did not

answer, and he began to worry. Nervously
attempting to avoid a panic attack, he decided to
take Zoso for a walk.

Zoso is very special to Jimmy. Joe bought
him shortly after he had to bury Buck—Jimmy's
Norwegian Dwarf Rabbit. A couple of years ago, on
a gorgeous Saturday in May, Joe and Lynn took
Jimmy to the "Land of Little Horses," in
Gettysburg, PA, mainly for nostalgic reasons. They
had taken Jenny and Jack there when they were
youngsters, but they never took Jimmy. Joe
premeditatedly decided to take the scenic route
home, and he intentionally stopped at Noah's Ark—a
pet shop Joe and Lynn had visited, many years ago,
which specialized in hard to get "designer dogs."
Jimmy wanted to see a miniature Pug, but they did
not have one. Nevertheless, each of them seemed
to be drawn to an adorable "designer dog" created
by a cross between a Toy Poodle and a miniature
Fox Terrier that was being bullied by an older
Chihuahua. Joe politely asked to see the puppy,
and the salesperson quickly complied. Jimmy was
standing adjacent to Joe when the salesperson
brought the eight-week old male puppy out for them
to see and hold. When Jimmy reached to pet the
tiny canine cradled in the salesperson's
arms, the precious puppy tenderly licked his face.
It was love at first lick. Joe impulsively bought
him, and everything else they needed to make him

feel comfortable in his new home. A few days later, they mutually agreed on Zoso as the name for the most welcomed addition to their household.

After taking Zoso for a short walk, Joe gave him a treat and nervously pressed the speed-dial number on his cell phone to call Lynn. It was 3:43 AM, and she finally answered. Joe said, "I've been trying to call you for more than half an hour." Happy to hear his voice, she sarcastically responded, "Verizon's so-called network must not be very reliable everywhere in the R. Adams Cowley Shock Trauma Center." Then, she quickly changed her tune saying, "I have no new news, but it's very comforting to know that everyone got home safely." Joe emotionally responded, "Please try to get some rest, and know that I love you." Lynn said, "I love you more," and quickly flipped her phone shut—a single tear tenderly traced a curvy path down the right side of her tired face. She took a deep breath, to compose herself, and was finally able to lie down and get some desperately needed rest.

Simultaneously, Joe went into the living room, sat down in his favorite chair, and turned the TV on. He just sat there, chain-smoking Marlboro lights, and blankly stared at the TV. A little less than one hour later—he stumbled up the stairs, tried to set the alarm, and crawled into bed.

At around 4:30 AM, Lynn suddenly arose and went to the TRU's waiting area to ask the receptionist to check on Jimmy. The receptionist phoned Jimmy's nurse in the TRU. They spoke briefly and, with very compassionate eyes, she said, "Nothing has changed." Lynn politely thanked her and began pacing again. While she was pacing, she was mentally taking note of the other people in the waiting area and wondering what they were experiencing. In the meantime, she noticed that the receptionist was strictly enforcing the two visitors at a time rule and began to nervously wonder why she let the four of them go back to see Jimmy. She began to panic and started thinking the worst again. Lynn's panic attack kept her pacing for almost an hour. An alertly concerned receptionist approached her and caringly suggested, "This might be a good time to get a cup of coffee and something to eat." Lynn appreciatively said, "Thank you," but fearful of leaving the waiting area, she ignored her thoughtful suggestion and continued to pace. After another solid hour of pacing, at around 6:30 AM, Lynn had calmed herself down enough to leave the TRU's waiting area and get a cup of coffee. She did not feel like eating, but she was craving a cup of coffee and a cigarette. She was pleasantly surprised to discover that a small hospital café served Starbuck's coffee. She ordered a cup of

their House Blend, paid for it, and immediately
returned to the TRU's waiting area to sip it and
anxiously await some news on Jimmy's condition.
The cigarette she was craving was unusually moved
to the last thing on her mind. As she slowly
sipped her cup of coffee, she briefly thought of
home—where she wanted to be—but her unfamiliar
surroundings quickly reminded her of where she was
and why she was there.

At exactly 7:00 AM, the TRU's receptionist
calmly approached her and said, "You can see your
son when you're ready." Lynn took a deep breath,
tried her best to remain calm, and casually walked
through the dreaded doors that stood between her
and her youngest son. He looked the same as he did
six hours ago. The same doctors, who were there at
that time, were busy focusing their attention on
several computer monitors and sharing their
thoughts. Jimmy's TRU nurse greeted her with a
genuine smile. A couple of doctors nodded to
acknowledge her presence. Lynn appreciatively
nodded back and nervously approached a still-
unconscious Jimmy, trying her best to hold back
the tears. It was very hard for her to look at
him, because it just made her feel worse. She
involuntarily decided to focus on her
surroundings, where she quietly observed that the
TRU was completely full and everyone there was
very busy. She keenly noticed that more patients

in critical condition were being brought in by both ambulance and helicopter. While all of that was happening, Jimmy's doctors stayed focused on the monitors they were viewing and continued sharing their observations with each other. Shortly thereafter, Jimmy's attending physician approached Lynn and said, "Your son sustained a traumatic brain injury, and I am going to move him into a private room, on the critical care floor, later today. Do you have any questions?" She politely replied, "Please, just keep me informed." He quickly answered, "Mrs. Masden, I can assure you that we will not just keep you informed—you will become an important part of the healing process." It was almost 11:30 AM and she began to worry, because Joe was not there.

The alarm clock, Joe thought he set, did not go off. However, after about three and a half hours of restless sleep, at around 9:00 AM, he somehow awoke on his own. He immediately observed the time and rushed downstairs to make a pot of coffee. Then, he went back upstairs to quickly shower, brush his teeth, and get dressed. Dazed and confused about everything that was happening, he went back downstairs, poured himself a cup of coffee, and took Zoso out for his morning potty-walk. After they returned, he drank his cup of coffee and unsuccessfully attempted to reach Lynn on her cell phone. Feeling a sense of urgency—he quickly downed a second cup of coffee and gently placed Zoso in his crate. Then, he grabbed a carton of cigarettes and left to drive Lynn's car back to the vaguely familiar hospital where he had left her and his critically injured son. While he was driving on Interstate 70 East, he tried to call Lynn's cell phone and failed to reach her. Not knowing what to think, he decided to focus on safely getting to the hospital. He successfully arrived, and parked in the hospital's parking garage at around 10:45 AM. After which, he jogged to the hospital, maneuvered through the revolving front door that would become so familiar to him, checked-in at the front desk to get his badge, and quickly made his way back to the shock trauma center. He immediately approached the receptionist and politely asked, "May I please see my son in the TRU?" She assertively replied, "We are extremely busy today. Please take a seat in the waiting area, and I will get back with you." Joe painfully honored her request.

He anxiously sat in the waiting area for more than thirty minutes. Then, he saw Lynn walking out of the TRU. Their eyes met. He rushed to her—gave her a kiss and a hug and inquired about Jimmy's status. She hugged him back and said, "I need a cigarette." As they were walking to the front of the hospital, she said, "Jimmy is holding his own and fighting. The doctor told me that he has a traumatic brain injury, and they are going to move him to a critical care room sometime later today."

They satisfied their nicotine addiction in the hospital's designated smoking area, and quickly made there way back to the TRU. Joe immediately noticed that Jimmy looked the same as he did when he left him. He had to force himself to refrain from crying, as he worriedly gazed upon the motionless body of his severely battered son, and all of the medical equipment that was apparently keeping him alive. He was wondering if Jimmy even had the slightest chance to recover and resume living a normal life. His pessimistic thoughts were agonizingly telling him that it was impossible for a 158-pound teenager, struck by a two-ton SUV going more than 40 mph, to still be living 15 hours later—let alone survive and recover. He was very anxious to hear, first-hand, what Jimmy's doctors could tell him about his son's current condition and their prognosis. He would have to wait a little while to get his answers.

It was almost noon and they had not had anything to eat. Instinctively, Joe and Lynn reluctantly decided to get something for lunch. They knew they were going to have a difficult time leaving their son, but they wanted to believe that they needed to be there for him when he recovered.

They decided to share a sub and a diet soda from a
Subway that was conveniently located adjacent to
the TRU. They did not enjoy their sub, but they
ate it anyway. Then they took, what would soon
become very familiar to them, "the walk" to the
designated smoking area. While they were standing
there—smoking their cigarettes and observing the
hustle and bustle—Joe broke the silence with a
fairly logical suggestion. Anxiously wanting to
ascertain the advice of a trusted medical
professional, he asked Lynn to contact Jimmy's
pediatrician. Lynn consented immediately and used
her cell phone to call the office of the
pediatrician that had cared for each of their
children from their births to the present time—a
span of more than 22 years. She had to leave a
message for her to return her call as soon as
possible. Then, they complacently decided to go
back to the TRU and spend some potentially
precious moments with their son.

Shortly after they returned, his nurse told
them that he was stable enough to move to their
intensive care brain trauma unit on the 4th floor,
and they were just waiting for a room to become
available. A few moments later, they were
approached by his admitting physician. He abruptly
said, "Jimmy has a closed head injury with a
traumatic subdural and intracranial hemorrhage;
punctuate lesions consistent with diffuse axonal

injury, and left-sided periorbital swelling." Joe
humbly requested a simplification. He said, "His
brain is injured and I may have to drill a hole in
his head to relieve the pressure from the
swelling. He has to be on a ventilator because he
is suffering from respiratory distress and his
lungs are bruised. He also had a small, but deep,
laceration in his left eyebrow, which I stitched
in accordance with the latest procedures followed
by the best plastic surgeons. Every organ in his
body, other than his heart and kidneys, sustained
bruises." Joe asked him if anything was broken. He
replied, "There are some sub-hairline fractures in
three of his lumbar vertebrae, which will not
require any treatment. Other than that—there are
no broken bones. I am somewhat concerned about a
mild thickening of his small intestine and the
pneumonia he contracted when he inhaled some vomit
that was probably initiated by the nasotracheal
intubation administered at the scene of the
accident. However, I am mostly concerned with a
small dissection flap that has narrowed the
diameter of one of his carotid arteries." A very
worried Lynn instantly asked for an explanation.
He replied, "One of the main arteries in his neck,
which transports blood to his brain, is blocked by
internal arterial tissue that has separated from
the inside of the artery's wall." Then, he proudly
revealed, "We developed the technology to diagnose

and treat this specific type of injury, almost ten years ago, but we are perplexed by the fact that he is only sixteen. Several doctors on the team, myself included, sternly believe that, because of his age, it might heal itself. However, we cannot locate a precedence to support our notion, and it is still an issue under discussion." Lynn asked, "What is Jimmy's current overall condition?" He answered, "He is stable enough to move to the intensive care unit, but only time will tell us how to proceed." Joe silently reminded himself that patience was a virtue.

At around 2:30 PM, they took "the walk," alluded to earlier, and Lynn checked her cell phone for any voice-mails. There was one voice-mail, from Jimmy's pediatrician, with a cell phone number and a request to contact her. Lynn phoned her and told her everything she knew about Jimmy's accident and his current condition. She strongly advised Lynn to keep him where he was; agree to any tests or treatments recommended by the doctors; and keep her informed. Lynn thanked her, assured her that she would, and ended the call. A few seconds later, Lynn's cell phone rang and she quickly answered. The caller was Jack, who was working very hard to get in shape at football camp. She decided not to tell him about his brother's accident because football camp was ending the next day, and the last thing she wanted to do was upset him. They briefly engaged in a conversation related to a dinner and a movie that he was going to with the football team, and said their good-byes. Less than a minute later, Lynn received a second phone call from Jack. He anxiously said, "Don just called me to ask how Jimmy was doing." Lynn cringingly felt like she had no choice but to tell him what had happened to his younger brother. She very reluctantly shared the details of how little she knew at the time, quickly ended the call, and immediately returned, with Joe, to the TRU.

A room in the intensive care brain trauma unit, located on the 4th floor of the shock trauma center, became available at around 5:00 PM. Joe and Lynn took the elevator to the 4th floor and nervously paced together in the waiting room. Shortly thereafter, Jimmy was paraded passed them in his hospital bed. A curious tingling emanated from Joe's spine and spread to his head and arms as Jimmy's apparently lifeless body went through the electronically monitored doorway that led to his private room. The tingling sensation subsided, and Joe inferred that an ethereal presence was there to watch over him. Consequentially, he silently, and elatedly, experienced a soothing feeling of relief.

After the doors closed, Joe and Lynn decided to get something to eat while Jimmy's intensive care nurse stabilized him in his new surroundings. They got some "to-go" food at an independent restaurant located on the hospital's first floor, and rushed to one of the benches situated in a park above the hospital's parking garage. They rather quickly consumed what they both considered to be a tasteless meal, and anxiously re-entered the hospital to see how Jimmy was doing. They cautiously walked into his critical care room at around 6:00 PM. Jimmy's battered body appeared to be resting comfortably. His nurse casually approached them and said, "He is stable; and he will be cared for by our "Team B" group of doctors. You should consider yourselves very fortunate, because they are second to none when it comes to motivating patients to fight to get their life back. Do you have any questions?" Lynn answered, "No, we just want to spend some time with him."

After they felt confident that Jimmy was stable enough for them to leave—Lynn obtained the phone numbers and contact information she would need to keep in touch with his nurse. Her maternal instinct told her to check on his condition before she tried to go to bed, and again in the morning. Then, they made their way to the underground parking garage, located their car and began

driving home. Shortly after exiting the Baltimore
beltway and driving a few miles on I-70 West, Lynn
phoned Jenny with an update. She simply said,
"Don't worry. Jimmy was moved into a private room,
and I truly believe that he is going to recover."
Jenny was speechless. She saw her brother on the
night it happened, and it was very hard for her to
believe that survival was even an option.

At around 8:00 PM, they arrived at their
house in Woodsville. One of Jimmy's concerned
friends was sitting on their front porch. Lynn
felt as if she had to convince him that Jimmy was
still alive. He was shaking his head in disbelief
as he slowly meandered down the sidewalk away from
their home. Joe retrieved a note stuck in the
storm door and placed it on the kitchen table.
Then, he went upstairs to wash his face, brush his
teeth, and change into his nightclothes. Lynn took
Zoso out for a potty-walk. After they returned,
she read the note that Joe left on the kitchen
table. It was from the young man who had alerted
them with the news of Jimmy's accident. He wanted
someone to contact him with an update. Lynn called
him and said, "Jimmy is still alive, and I am very
optimistic." He was very pleased with the good
news, and promised to relay it to the rest of his
worried family. Then, Lynn picked-up the newspaper
and read the following article that was printed on

page 6 of the Friday, August 25, edition of The
Woodsville Ledger.

Pedestrian Struck by Policeman

WOODSVILLE – A teenage pedestrian was struck by an
SUV on Md. 176 near Bluestone Drive about 9 p.m. Thursday,
Maryland State Police said.

The teen was running across Md. 176 when he was struck by a
2003 Chevy Blazer driven by Adam Grove, 25, of Midway. Mr.
Grove is a Maryland State Policeman and was not on duty at the
time.

Police were unsure if the pedestrian would survive the
injuries. The victim was flown to R. Adams Cowley Shock
Trauma Center in Baltimore by a Maryland State Police
helicopter.

Preliminary investigation showed the pedestrian was at
fault, and neither speed nor alcohol were a factor.

Reconstruction crews and the Frederick County State's
Attorney's Office were on the scene of the crash Thursday
night to gather evidence.

- Edna Lucci

After reading the very disturbing news, Lynn
went upstairs to change into her bedclothes. Then,
overcome with anxiety, she returned to phone the
grandparents. Telling them that one of their
grandchildren had been hit by an SUV, and was
fighting for his life in the shock trauma unit of
a Baltimore hospital was not going to be an easy
task. At approximately 9:00 PM, Lynn called Joe's
father and he was rendered speechless by the
shocking news. Lynn emotionally left him with the
assurance that she would stay in touch. Then, she
phoned her parents to share the same disheartening
news, and got the same sound of silence. She could

only promise to keep them informed, and end the
call with tears in her eyes.

Lynn's mother was instinctively propelled
into action. She immediately got on the phone to
start a prayer chain which, along with the similar
action initiated by some of Joe's colleagues,
quickly covered almost all of Virginia. She also
contacted relatives in West Virginia and Georgia,
who caringly started praying for Jimmy. Then, she
called Lynn back to tell her what she had done. It
began to occur to Joe that, in a state of panic,
truly caring human beings turned to God—to pray
for his will to be done and then cope with what
faith told them was His decision. He could not
have agreed more with what he perceived to be
sincerely honest intentions, and he was very
appreciative of their decision to pray, along with
him, for what he did not want to believe was
impossible.

The answering machine was blinking. The
message was from one of Joe's concerned
colleagues. He returned the call, gave his co-
worker an update, and asked for a favor. He needed
his out-of-state principal's phone number. The
friendly colleague gave him the phone number and
wished him well. He immediately phoned his
principal. After hearing the horrific news, she
replied, "Don't worry about work. I will get a
very capable substitute to cover for you. Everyone

here will be very understanding. You need to focus on your son and your family. Please email me, or my secretary, with any updates. We will keep each of you in our prayers." With tears welling-up in his eyes, Joe politely thanked her and quietly ended the conversation.

At approximately 10:30 PM, Lynn phoned Jimmy's nurse to ascertain any change in his condition. His nurse told her that everything was still the same. Jimmy was sedated, intubated, and subconsciously fighting for his life. Still in a state of shock, Joe and Lynn tried to get some rest, but rest was for the weary. They closed their eyes and prayed until the alarm clock alerted them to the fact that it was time to prepare for another rising sun that never rose before.

CHAPTER 7: SHOCKED AGAIN

The dawning of a new day meant that it was time for Lynn to make some coffee and call the shock trauma center to check on Jimmy. Nothing had changed. They drank their coffee, and drove straight to the hospital. Joe parked in the underground parking garage and they quickly took the usual route to their son's room. It was very reminiscent of the day before—Jimmy was still unconscious and fighting for his life. However, because he was still alive, a bright glimmer of promising hope took refuge in their hearts.

They were quite impressed by the fact that it was a Saturday, and the staff was operating as if it were a weekday. Before and after a lunch break, they emotionally spent a few hours talking to their sedated, unconscious son and lovingly touched him; wishfully hoping that he could somehow sense their presence. After they returned from an early afternoon cigarette break, they were pleasantly surprised to see a semi-awake Jimmy sitting in a chair. His right eye was open and he appeared to recognize them, but the only response they could get was a thumbs-up made with his left hand. He obviously could not move his right side and they were very concerned that it might be paralyzed.

His pulmonary technician came in to see him. She said, "He's doing great. I am going to start weaning him off the ventilator." After she left, they took a late afternoon cigarette break, while his nurse moved him back into his hospital bed. When they returned, his right eye was still open and he was moving his left arm and leg. His nurse asked him to give her a thumbs-up a couple of times, and he slowly responded using only his left hand. It appeared to Lynn that he was somewhat reluctantly responding to her request and curiously suggested, "Try asking for a peace sign." She respectfully complied, and Jimmy quickly flashed a peace sign.

After his nurse left, to check on her other patients, Joe and Lynn took turns asking Jimmy for a thumbs-up and a peace sign. He always gave the correct response, but he definitely seemed to prefer the request for the peace sign, because he always responded to it much faster. They would find out later, when Lynn called from home to get an update, that there was a fairly benign request that would render an even faster response.

When the time came for them to leave again, they were very worried and concerned—because Jimmy's nurse had medicated him, and he was, once again, rendered unconscious. All the way home, Lynn was praying that his somewhat limited response to her presence was intrinsically related to the healing process.

Joe and Lynn had initiated a routine, upon arriving in Woodsville, that they would maintain throughout their son's hospital stay. After they arrived, they stopped at Wawa to fill the car with gas and drove, less than one-half mile, to their house. Shortly after they entered, Lynn took Zoso out for a potty-walk and Joe retrieved the mail. Then, they went upstairs and changed into their bedclothes. The completion of those mundane tasks brought them back downstairs to read the mail, listen and respond to any messages that were left on their answering machine, and check for any emails.

One of Lynn's emails, from a very religious Catholic co-worker, captured her attention. Her concerned co-worker had contacted a worldwide prayer organization, known as the "Prayer Warriors," and she informed her that they would be praying for Jimmy all over the world—which included the Vatican in Rome. Lynn shared her co-worker's virtuous act of kindness with Joe, and he was both very impressed with her thoughtful action and thankful that so many people believed in the power of prayer.

They went into the living room, turned the TV on, and tried to relax until it was time for

Lynn to phone their parents with the day's news.
At around 9:00 PM, She phoned their parents with
an optimistic update. They were cautiously
relieved, promised their prayers, and caringly
requested that she keep them informed. Lynn
assured them that she would.

At exactly 10:00 PM, Lynn phoned Jimmy's
nurse for an update. His nurse told her that he
was stable and variably responding to her
commands. She was chuckling when she said, "He
stopped responding to my request for a thumbs-up,
so I asked him to give me "the finger" and he
instantly responded." Lynn smiled for the first
time in three days; and, after she hung the phone
up, quite giddily shared that exciting bit of news
with Joe. Joe felt somewhat comforted, disturbed,
and elated at the same time. Then, they kissed
each other goodnight, and went to bed.

They crawled out of bed at 7:00 AM and began
their morning ritual. Lynn started a pot of coffee
and took Zoso out for a potty-walk. Joe smoked a
cigarette. At 7:35 AM, they were dressed and
sitting at the kitchen table—smoking cigarettes
and sipping their first cup of coffee. Lynn
skimmed the Sunday paper. The Woodsville Ledger
ran a second article related to Jimmy's accident.

State's attorney investigating crash

WOODSVILLE – The Frederick County State's Attorney's

Office expects to wrap up, by the end of next week, its investigation of a pedestrian struck on Md. 176 near Bluestone Drive on Thursday night, according to state's attorney Roy Minter.

"It appears to be pedestrian error," Mr. Minter said. "The investigation is ongoing."

About 8:45 p.m. Thursday, a teenager attempting to cross Md. 176 was struck by a 2003 Chevy Blazer driven by Andrew Grove, 25, of Midway according to Maryland State Police. Mr. Grove is a Maryland State Policeman but was not on duty at the time of the crash.

The state's attorney's office was called to the scene because a police officer was involved in the crash, Mr. Minter said.

Speed and alcohol were not factors in the crash, according to police.

- Edna Lucci

Lynn phoned Jimmy's nurse at 8:00 AM for an update. She simply said, "He's holding his own, and still fighting." At 9:15 AM, they began their now familiar commute to the hospital's underground parking garage. They walked into Jimmy's ICU room just before 11:00 AM, and his day-nurse immediately approached them with some encouraging news. He said, "Your son's pneumonia is healing, his breathing has improved, and he has been opening his right eye on a regular basis. His left eye is just badly bruised and swollen shut." Lynn asked, "Could you wake him up so we could talk to him." He assuredly replied, "His doctor has ordered us to wake him and wean him off the ventilator." She curiously asked, "What should we expect?" He answered, "Life would be so much easier if these things happened as they were portrayed on television—where the patient

miraculously reverts to their normal self. Jimmy
will question you about why he is here, and what
happened to him, on his time. When the time is
right, it will be as if someone flipped a light-
switch on in his brain, and he will want to know
what happened to him."

A couple of hours later, Joe and Lynn
desperately tried to find hope—as the nurse
weaned their son from the medication that was
keeping him in a coma-like state. He began moving
his left side over to his apparently immobile
right side, in a flailing-like motion, as he began
to "wake up." When he was somewhat coherent, his
pulmonary technician disconnected the breathing
machine that was helping to keep him alive. He
responded very well to the final weaning process,
and she decided to remove the tube that had been
supplying him with oxygen for a little more than
three days.

Joe and Lynn took "the walk" while she
removed the tube, and Lynn phoned their parents
with the good news. When they returned, Jimmy was
semi-awake and sitting in a chair. An oxygen mask
had replaced the uncomfortable tracheal tube. He
appeared to be incoherent, which was only a side
effect of the medication they gave him to
facilitate the removal of the irritating tube.

Shortly afterwards, Jimmy's nurse
informatively said, "We are racing the clock

to get him well enough to be transferred to another facility. We want to move him to intermediate care later today—if he successfully maintains his oxygen saturation level. Intermediate care is a step-up from intensive care and he will not get the same amount of attention."

Joe did not think that Jimmy was ready to be moved, because he had not asked them why he was there. He just kept saying that he was thirsty. Lynn asked his nurse if she could give him something to drink. The nurse told her that he could not drink any liquids from a glass, but she could dip sterilized sponge lollipops in cold water and put them in his mouth to help quench his thirst. Lynn immediately secured a stash of sponge lollipops and began using them as the nurse had instructed. Jimmy appeared to be grateful, because he kept asking for more.

It was nearly 4:00 PM when his doctors gave the orders. His vital signs were stable, and he was much more alert than he had been for the past three days. His nurse had finally gotten a positive response when he tested Jimmy's right side for movement, and a doctor corroborated the nurse's findings. They agreed that he was substantially weaker on his right side, but they definitely witnessed a positive response and were very optimistic. Therefore, Jimmy was moved to intermediate care on the hospital's sixth floor.

Lynn was somewhat excited—but, Joe was very
concerned about the fact that Jimmy had not asked
them why he was there.

When they visited him in his new room, they
noticed that the nurses were younger, and even
though they were assigned to more patients, they
appeared to be less-stressed than the ICU nurses.
It was reminiscent of the typical hospital
atmosphere they had become accustomed to over the
years—where the patients are healing, rather than
fighting for their lives.

Jimmy's room was situated directly across
from the nurses' station and he was resting
comfortably. His nurse came in to introduce
herself. They calmly reciprocated and asked her
what they should expect. She replied, "Jimmy will
not be monitored as closely as he was in the ICU.
However, because it's his first night here, we
will check on him more often than usual." In
unison, they both said, "Thank you," and the nurse
left. It was close to dinnertime, so they decided
to get something to eat and take "the walk".

When they returned, Jimmy still appeared to
be resting comfortably. They took turns holding
his hand and talking to him, but he did not
respond. Joe focused his attention on the digital
equipment that displayed his vital signs, because
he was very worried that it was too soon to move

him. However, now that the deed was done, he sensibly tried his best to support the decision.

The time passed quickly, and it was time for them to leave again. Lynn secured the pertinent contact information from Jimmy's nurse, and told her to expect a phone call at 10:00 PM. They took turns kissing their son on his forehead, telling him that they loved him, and left to go home at 7:00 PM. When they reached I-70 West, Lynn phoned Jenny with an update. After they exited I-70 West for Route 15 North, Joe asked Lynn if he could stop at Walmart to buy a CD player. To convince her, he brought up their excursion to NYC, earlier in the summer, and Jimmy's apparent infatuation with John Lennon and his music. Then, he said, "Exposing Jimmy to music he likes might inspire him to come back to us." Lynn curiously agreed, and they stopped at Walmart to purchase a CD player. Joe decided on a Sony clock radio that played CD's and they went home.

They entered their house, and followed their established routine. Lynn was anxiously waiting until 9:00 PM to call their parents. While she was waiting, Joe went upstairs, to Jimmy's room, to look for CDs that he could bring with him the next day. He chose John Lennon's "Imagine" and the "Best of John Lennon." He also found a clear double CD case that would perfectly house both CDs. Then, he went back downstairs to write

Jimmy's name on the CD case and put it in the box
that contained his new CD/clock radio. At 9:00 PM,
Lynn made the usual phone calls to update their
concerned parents. After which, they went back
into the living room to blankly stare at the
television until it was time to call their son's
nurse for an update. At 10:00 PM, Lynn made the
call and nothing had changed. They went to bed,
only to toss and turn, until the alarm clock
alerted them that it was time to start all over.

They awoke feeling hopeful, and calmly
followed their established morning ritual. Lynn
phoned Jimmy's nurse at 8:00 AM to get an update.
She said, "He's doing very well. He's still
breathing on his own, and everything appears to be
moving in the right direction."

They left for Baltimore at 9:30 AM, in
accordance with Joe's pre-meditated attempt to
avoid the morning rush-hour traffic. While they
were waiting for the red light to change, at the
intersection of Slater Road and Route 176, Joe
turned the radio on. The Beatles, "Let It Be,"
began playing. They were quietly listening to
every word when the light turned green, and Joe
made the left turn onto Route 176 South. "When I
find myself in times of trouble - Mother Mary
comes to me - Speaking words of wisdom - Let it
be." The trip was otherwise uneventful, and they

successfully pulled into the hospital's underground parking garage around 11:00 AM.

They were very excited about Jimmy's apparently successful move to intermediate care, and they could not wait to see him. Joe anxiously pushed the 6th floor button on the panel of the first elevator that was going up. The elevator quickly reached its destination and the doors quietly opened. Joe and Lynn exited and took a double-right-turn around the corner into the main hallway. Joe pressed the square button on the right-side wall, to alert the nurse's station that they wanted to gain entrance. The electronically controlled doors opened and they hastily paced to the room where they had left their son.

He was not there—and their hearts began to race. His bed was gone, and because of the room's untidy appearance, Joe assumed that he was rushed out of there. The queasy feeling in his stomach confirmed his rapid progression into a bona fide state of shock. Lynn was experiencing the same gut-wrenching sensation.

A nurse quickly entered the room, and said, "Jimmy was having trouble breathing, and his doctor decided to reintubate him." Unfortunately, that meant he was put back on the ventilator they had just weaned him from yesterday. Joe and Lynn were visibly distraught and painfully devastated. The flustered nurse said, "Please have a seat. Can

I bring you some water?" They sat down and kindly declined her offer for water. Lynn calmly asked, "Where is our son?" She replied, "He is downstairs in the TRU holding area, and a nurse is checking to see if it is all right for you to go down there."

Less than five minutes later, a nurse was leading them to an elevator that would transport them down to the TRU's holding area—where Jimmy was closely being monitored and unconsciously waiting for an open room. They were still in a state of shock when they saw their sedated son. He was back on the life support system that he was weaned from yesterday, and they were very concerned for his life.

The following account of this episode was written in his doctor's report.

> "During the patient's hospital course he was extubated and transferred out of the ICU; however, the following day there was a decrease in his mental status and some respiratory difficulty. Patient was subsequently reintubated by anesthesia and had a stat head CT which, however, was stable and showed no interval worsening of his closed head injury. At the time, patient was subsequently transferred back to the ICU for further management."
> "In addition, during that time, patient had a CAT scan of his chest to rule out a PE secondary to his decompensation. It did not show any evidence of PE however it did show what was concerning for a pneumonia. There was a left lower lobar pneumonia noted on CT scan of his chest and patient was subsequently started on antibiotics for that."

Translated into layman's language—the incident could be simplified as follows:

Jimmy was taken off of the ventilator and transferred out of intensive care. The next day he was having trouble breathing. Therefore, he had to be put back on the ventilator and transferred back into intensive care. His doctor ordered CAT scans of his head and chest to rule out worsening of his head injury, a blood clot in a lung, and pneumonia. It was determined that he had pneumonia in his left lung, and he was put on medicine to treat it.

CHAPTER 8:   GET YOUR LENNON ON

Jimmy was quickly moved back into a private room on shock trauma's 4th floor ICU. He was classified as stable; but, he was assigned a personal nurse—"just to be on the safe side." Joe and Lynn arrived shortly after they had settled him in his new room. He was heavily sedated, but his vital signs looked good.

Joe showed the clock radio/CD player to Jimmy's nurse and asked, "Can I play music for my son?" The nurse replied, "Yes, many patients' families have done the same thing for their loved ones." Joe located an open electrical outlet, plugged it in, and started playing John Lennon's "Imagine" CD. Jimmy appeared to be unresponsive, but Joe reasoned that he might be listening. After the last song played, Joe switched to the "Best of John Lennon" CD and he kept the music playing, flip-flopping CDs, until it was time go home.

When the time came to leave, Jimmy was still unconscious. Joe anxiously asked his nurse, "Could you keep playing music all night long?" The nurse smiled and said, "I will keep it playing while I'm on duty, and I will relay your request to his night-nurse when we change shifts."

The ride home was quiet and uneventful. After arriving, they simply followed their established routine. Lynn phoned their parents

with the disheartening news, and she confidently
told each of them, "It's just a minor setback."
Joe firmly believed that she was trying more to
convince herself, than she was their parents.

At 10:00 PM, Lynn called Jimmy's night-nurse
for an update. She said, "Everything is about the
same. Jimmy is stable. His vital signs look good,
and he is resting comfortably." Lynn asked, "Are
you playing the music?" She happily replied, "Yes,
and I will keep playing it through the night."
Lynn thanked her and politely ended the
conversation.

She started to tell Joe what the nurse had
said, but she noticed flurry of tears caressing
his blushing cheeks that put her on pause. He
began blaming himself for the accident. "I never
showed Jimmy enough love and I am so sorry. I know
it's my fault, and I am so sorry. Please give me
another chance. Dear God, please give me another
chance. I promise, with all my heart, that I won't
let you down. I will show him how much I love
him." Lynn could tell that his tears were real,
and she felt a little bit jealous because she
wanted to let her feelings out, but she was still
too pumped-up with adrenaline and maternal
instinct.

On Tuesday, the 29th of August, they once
again maneuvered through all the routine motions
that safely brought them to the hospital's

underground parking garage. Surprisingly, the garage was full and the attendant gave them directions to another parking garage conveniently located a few blocks away. They easily found it, but it was not easy to find a parking space. They ended up parking on the roof with a view that was rather comforting. It was partly cloudy, warm, and humid. The National Weather Service predicted that severe thunderstorms, with the possibility of tornadoes, would arrive later in the afternoon. They located the elevator; and, it felt weird to be taking it down, because they had become accustomed to taking the elevator up for the past five days.

They quickly walked to the hospital, got their passes, and cautiously entered Jimmy's room shortly after 11:00 AM. He was still there, still sedated, and still on life support. One of the John Lennon CDs was softly playing. His nurse came in to record his vitals, and said, "His doctor wants to wean him from the ventilator again. It was probably the pneumonia that caused the difficulty he experienced yesterday." She went on to explain, "Because he is being treated for the pneumonia, he could be given oxygen through a mask if he needs it, but his doctor does not think that will be necessary. I am going to reduce his medication and "wake him up," so his respiratory therapist could do another evaluation and begin the weaning process."

They had just decided to leave and get something for lunch, when his respiratory therapist walked into the room. He said, "I've been monitoring Jimmy all morning, because I want to take him off the ventilator as soon as possible. I'm just here to see how he's doing." Joe turned the CD player off, and they patiently waited while he determined Jimmy's current status. He said, "He's doing very well—but, I would like to test him again, in a couple of hours, before I make my decision." They very appreciatively thanked him. Then, Joe restarted the CD player, and they left to get some lunch.

When they returned, Jimmy was sleeping and John Lennon's CD was still playing. The breathing and feeding tubes that were keeping him supplied with the oxygen and nutrients he needed to heal were in place and functioning. All of his vital signs were stable, but he still had a fever. They were becoming very good at reading the digital equipment that constantly monitored his pulse, blood pressure, breathing rate, oxygen level and body temperature. The Lennon CD played its last song and Joe got up to switch the player to a soft rock FM radio station.

Jimmy began to exhibit some signs of life at around 1:30 PM. He was opening his right eye and his left hand consistently responded to his parent's request for a peace sign. His respiratory therapist returned to see him at approximately 2:00 PM. He said, "Everything looks good. In all probability, I will be taking his breathing tube out tomorrow."

Joe and Lynn spent a relatively uneventful afternoon and early evening with their son. Joe just kept changing one Lennon CD for the other, switching to FM radio, and monitoring his vital signs. Lynn continuously spoke to him, while she held his hand and lovingly caressed his head. A catholic priest dropped by, introduced himself, and politely asked them if they would pray with him. They sincerely appreciated, and warmly welcomed, his thoughtful request. Joe turned the music off. They closed their eyes, and respectfully bowed their heads. He calmly said, "Almighty God, please watch over Jimmy and keep him in your grace. With your divine intervention, give his parents the strength they will need to care for him and assist him in starting his new life."

Jimmy's neurologist came in to see them shortly after the priest left. He reintroduced himself and said, "Jimmy's brain injury is progressing in a positive direction, as expected, but Team B is very concerned about his dissected carotid artery. A team of doctors is working on

developing a course of action, because their
research failed to yield an established treatment
plan for a 16-year-old with an identical injury.
The team's initial reaction was to put him on a
blood-thinning medication and monitor the
potential healing of the artery, because of his
age, by taking CT angiograms every couple of
months for up to one year." Joe immediately agreed
to that course of action, and politely asked,
"Could you please divulge some detailed
information related to any alternatives that the
team is considering?" He curiously replied, "Jimmy
was very fortunate that we found the injury as
early as we did; he was put on aspirin, to thin
his blood and reduce his chances for a potential
stroke, immediately after the diagnosis. Now, as I
have told you, some of the team members want to
put him on coumadin, a blood-thinning medication,
and monitor the injured artery via CT angiogram.
However, a few dissenting members of the team want
to place a stent in the artery, which is the
standard form of treatment for his type of injury
in older patients. The coumadin and monitor
faction is firmly against it. The stent would have
to be regularly monitored and replaced, when
necessary, as he got older. I appreciate your
input, and I will keep you fully informed." Then,
he shook Joe's hand, nodded to Lynn, and quietly
left.

Joe and Lynn decided to get something to eat. They hastily consumed another sub-par dinner in the hospital's cafeteria, after which, they took "the walk" and checked on the weather. The sky appeared ominous but nothing severe was happening.

When they returned to Jimmy's room—he was sleeping. They took turns talking to him, caressing his head, and holding his hand. Joe kept the music playing. When it was time for them to leave, Joe politely asked Jimmy's nurse if she would keep playing the music. She compassionately agreed, and promised that she would pass his request on to her replacement. They tearfully kissed their son goodnight, and quietly left to go home.

Joe almost forgot that they parked in a different parking garage, but they did not get very far before he remembered. Woefully, they walked the extra couple of blocks, and took the parking garage's elevator up to the roof to locate their car. They paused for a moment, to take in the view and observe the ominous sky, which still appeared to be threatening in all directions. Then, they quickly located their car and headed home. It had rained on and off throughout the day, and they drove through some showers on I-70 West, but they never got the severe weather that was predicted. After they arrived home, they flawlessly executed their routine. Lynn made the usual phone calls to update their parents, and waited until 10:00 PM to phone Jimmy's nurse. His nurse said, "Everything looks good, and I will keep the music playing."

CHAPTER 9: "A DAY TO REMEMBER"

Everything was going well on Wednesday the
30th of August. The weather was beautiful, the
8:00 AM report from Jimmy's nurse was very
positive, and Joe fortunately found a space in the
underground parking garage. They were excited, and
acting quite giddy, as they made their way from
the parking garage to the hospital. After they
stopped to get their passes, they felt as if they
were gliding down the hallway toward the elevator
that would take them up to their son in the ICU.

They could hear John Lennon singing as they
approached his room. "Imagine all the people –
Living life in peace – You could say I'm a dreamer
– But I'm not the only one – I hope someday you'll
join us – And the world can live as one." Jimmy
was awake when they entered his room and he
appeared to be more alert than he had been. He was
opening both eyes, and only using his left hand to
respond to their request for a peace sign, but Joe
keenly sensed that something was different. Joe
sat in a chair and observed, as Lynn caressed
Jimmy's head and held his left hand. She excitedly
told him about all the little things Zoso did last
night, and Jimmy appeared to be listening. He
tried his best to smile when he responded by
turning his head to look in the direction of
Zoso's picture that Joe had taped to the inside

panel of his bed. Lynn kept holding his hand and caressing his head, as she changed the subject of her one-sided conversation to the multitude of phone calls, cards, and emails they had been receiving from family, friends, and co-workers. Jimmy did not appear to be listening; the solemn look on his face silently informed Joe that something was bothering him.

Jimmy's respiratory therapist walked into the room. He had some exciting news to share with them. "For the most part," he said, "your son has been breathing on his own for the past 48 hours. When I put him back on the ventilator, he was only getting some pressure support; and, I reduced it to the lowest level around 24 hours ago. I am only here to check on his progress." After he read and recorded what the electronic monitors revealed, he confided, "I am going to report my findings to his doctor, who will probably tell me to take him off the ventilator later this afternoon." Joe and Lynn were afraid to get excited. The agonizing memory of the last time this crucial procedure was performed was still freshly imprinted in their minds.

Both of them were experiencing the jitters, as they took the elevator down to consume another hospital cafeteria lunch. It was probably the butterflies in their stomachs, not the cafeteria food, that limited their intake. They took "the walk," after eating what they thought they could keep down, and quickly returned to Jimmy's room.

His nurse was in his room, and she was smiling as they approached. Jimmy was not only awake—he was very alert. He obviously recognized them, because his eyes "lit up" with excitement. He immediately indicated to his mom, by making writing motions with his left hand, that he wanted to write something. Lynn quickly located a pencil and a piece of paper, and handed them to him. Right-handed Jimmy sloppily wrote something with his left hand, and gave the piece of paper to his mother. She could not decipher what he had written, so she just shrugged her shoulders. Jimmy motioned to her to give him the paper, and she curiously complied. He turned it over and slowly started writing again. His second attempt was much more legible. He wrote, "Why, how, where, who? Dave also?" Joe interpreted it as, "Why am I here?"; "How did I get here?"; "Where am I?"; "Who hurt me?"; "Is Dave hurt?"

Jimmy was back in a huge way and it happened exactly as his nurse had said it would several days ago. *"When the time is right; it will be as if someone flipped a light-switch on in his brain, and he will immediately want to know what had happened to him."* That was exactly what his parents had just witnessed, and it did not end there. Lynn had to give him several sheets of paper, which his nurse put on a clipboard, so he could continue to communicate with them.

Joe got the ball rolling with, "You were hit by an SUV, and you're in a hospital in Baltimore." Jimmy wanted to know if Dave was hurt. Lynn replied, "Dave was not injured." He immediately wrote, "Who hit me?". Joe answered, "It was an off-duty state policeman." Then, he wanted to know how badly he was hurt and why he could not move his right side. Joe said, "Your injuries are very serious, but the doctors believe that you will be able to move your right side when you're better." He wrote, "My head and right side hurt. How did I get here?" Joe answered, "You flew in a state police helicopter, and your nurse is giving you medicine to help with the pain." He wanted to know if Jenny had come to see him. Lynn responded, "Jenny and Bill came to see you on the night it happened." He wrote to tell his brother Jack that he was okay, not to worry about him, and to concentrate on college. Lynn replied, trying to hold back the tears, "I will call your brother and relay your message." Then, he wanted to know about Zoso. Lynn said, "Zoso is doing OK, but I could tell that he misses you—because he keeps going to your room to look for you." At that point, he wrote that he did not want to hear any more music because his head hurt. Joe said, "I won't play any more music." Then, he wanted to know what day it was. Lynn quickly replied, "It's Wednesday." He paused for a moment, and then wrote to ask her why they were there on a workday. Lynn thoughtfully said, "We took the day off, and we will continue to take days off until you are better." His written reply floored them, "Will you and dad take tomorrow and Friday off, and because Monday is Labor Day, I'll go back to school on Tuesday." Joe and Lynn were held speechless for a moment, not knowing whether to laugh or cry. Lynn quickly composed herself and said, "We will take the days off, but we'll have to make the back-to-school decision on Monday." He complained about the tube in his throat. Joe tried to comfort him saying, "It's helping you to breathe, and your doctor is going to remove it as soon as possible." He ended the session writing, "Tell my nurse that my head and right side hurts."

Joe immediately left to locate Jimmy's nurse. Shortly thereafter, she entered the room and quickly administered the pain medication. Jimmy suddenly became drowsy and dosed off. Joe and Lynn mutually decided that it would be a good time for them to take "the walk."

When they returned, Jimmy was drowsy and appeared to be resting comfortably. He would open both eyes when either of them spoke to him—but, for the most part, he was unresponsive. Lynn held his left hand and caressed his head. Joe sat in a chair and tried to relax for the first time in almost a week.

Shortly after 2:00 PM, Jimmy's nurse and respiratory therapist entered the room with some exciting news. His doctor signed the orders for him to be re-taken off the ventilator and they were there to remove the uncomfortable tube from his irritated trachea. Lynn anxiously asked, "What is the probability of the same thing that happened the last time happening again?" The respiratory therapist answered, "His doctor may have to perform a tracheotomy, but I am very confident that it won't be necessary. Will you and your husband take a break and come back in about an hour?" As they were leaving, Joe tried to reassure his wife saying, "Everything is going to be all right this time, because Jimmy is communicating with us." Lynn wanted to be optimistic for the very same reason, but the haunting memory of the previous extubation still irked her.

They exited the hospital through its revolving front door, and decided to take a walk. They took a right and walked until they reached Lombard Street—a relatively short distance from the stadiums where the Orioles and Ravens play their home games, and Baltimore's magnificent Inner Harbor. Joe spotted a police officer standing on the corner across the street, and suddenly felt an urge to talk to someone. He nonchalantly crossed the street and began speaking to the strange policeman. The policeman was all ears as Joe shared the short version of Jimmy's accident and their current situation. The policeman said, "Someone in heaven is looking out for you and your son." Joe shook his hand and humbly thanked him. Then, he quickly crossed the street to join Lynn. The mostly one-sided conversation had helped to calm his nerves. In his temporarily rejuvenated state of mind, the word impossible had a new meaning.

Joe and Lynn headed back to the hospital's main entrance. When they got there, Joe looked at his wristwatch and observed that they still had about half an hour to wait. They decided to search for an unoccupied bench, across the street, in the park that covered the roof of the underground parking garage. They located one and just sat there, quietly listening to the plethora of city sounds that surrounded them, while they silently contemplated what they could expect to learn in less than half an hour. The temperature was comfortable, the birds were chirping, a hurricane was threatening the Carolinas, and the time passed quickly.

Shortly before 3:00 PM, they anxiously began making their way back to Jimmy's room. When they arrived, he had an aerosol mask covering his nose and mouth, and he appeared to be quite drowsy. His nurse came in and said, "The procedure went quite well. You should expect him to be a little groggy for about another half hour, because he was mildly anesthetized." She paused for a moment and said, "His doctors are planning to move him back into Intermediate Care as soon as possible." Lynn panicked and quickly requested, "Please don't move him back to the 6ᵗʰ floor." She tried to comfort her saying, "In all probability, he will be moved to the Intermediate Care wing on this floor. Everyone is very well aware of what happened the last time." Lynn asked, "When do you expect it to happen?" She quickly answered, "By tomorrow at the latest."

Jimmy was now quite capable of oral communication. Lynn had apparently answered all of his questions earlier, because all he would talk about was the pain he was feeling and the fact that he could not move his right side. Joe tried to reassure him, "Your doctors told us that you will regain motion and control of your right side in time." Jimmy acted as if he wanted to believe him. Joe wondered about how the potent pain medication might be affecting his son's ability to sense the severe muscle and nerve damage he had sustained. Then, he remembered believing that the word impossible had a new meaning.

CHAPTER 10: MOVING IN THE RIGHT DIRECTION

It was just a week ago—when the frantic knock on the siding of their house initiated the all-too-real nightmare they were still experiencing. It was just a week ago—when they heard the dreadful news, went to the scene of the accident, and later found themselves viewing the severely battered body of their youngest child.

This Thursday would be much different than the last. Joe and Lynn followed their established routine and walked into Jimmy's new 4th floor Intermediate Care room, shortly before 11:00 AM, with an air of confidence. He had already been given a cognitive-linguistic evaluation and the overall results were very encouraging. He was fully awake and complaining about the pain he was feeling. The aerosol mask was replaced with nasal tubes, so he could use his mouth for speaking and eating. The nasal feeding tube had been removed, along with the catheter that had carried urine out of his bladder for the past week, and he was upgraded to a semi-solid diet and a bedpan. Unfortunately, he still had a fever.

One medical professional after another paraded into his room to either—check on him, collect data, perform tests, or engage him in some form of therapy. Each of them expressed their amazement with his progress. His medical team decided to put him on a heparin drip, to thin his blood, and prepare him for a changeover to warfarin. They were very concerned about his dissected carotid artery.

His nurse approached Joe and Lynn in the middle of the afternoon and said, "We are making plans to move your son to a local hospital that specializes in the rehabilitation of patients who are recovering from brain injuries. You should expect a visit from his social worker within the hour." Lynn asked, "Is he really ready to be moved?" She confidently replied, "I am absolutely certain."

Joe and Lynn anxiously went back into Jimmy's room, and he was working with his physical therapist. She was telling them how well he was doing when, as promised, they were suddenly approached by his social worker. She walked them to a nearby conference room and immediately began giving them their options. She was very pleasant and seemed to enjoy her position in the systemic hierarchy that had obviously been established long before they arrived on the scene. She finally said, "I strongly recommend that he be moved to Sherman Hospital. It's just a few miles North of here, off of Interstate 70, and it is part of the University of Maryland Medical System. All of his files and insurance information could very easily be transferred." Lynn quickly asked, "Is the staff

at Sherman Hospital more than just adequately
capable of rehabilitating our son?" She answered,
"I have no doubt. The medical staff and therapists
rank among the best in the state when it comes to
rehabilitating patients with traumatic brain
injuries." Lynn asked, "How soon can you move
him?" She replied, "He is definitely ready, and
the move could take place as early as tomorrow—if
I can secure an open bed."

The first of September would be much more
than just another first. It was going to be the
first time, in more than a week, that Jimmy would
truly see the light of day. Lynn made her usual
8:00 AM call to Jimmy's nurse, and the news was
better than good. His nurse said, "He slept
through the night, and I am very confident that he
is ready to be transferred. By the time you and
your husband arrive, solidified plans to move him
to Sherman Hospital will be well underway."

They arrived close to 11:00 AM and Jimmy was
being treated by one of his therapists. She said,
"He's doing great. This is the second time that I
have been in to treat him this morning. I know
that he's been scheduled to be transferred early
this afternoon and I want to send an accurate up-
to-date report to the hospital."

Shortly before 1:30 PM, there was a
commotion in the hallway just outside of Jimmy's
room. It was the on-time arrival of the qualified

medical transfer team. They quickly took care of
the paperwork, and professionally prepped Jimmy
for his relatively short trip to the next stop on
his way home. Before they knew it, Joe and Lynn
were anxiously heading in the direction of the car
they had parked in the hospital's underground
parking garage. Jimmy was being taken, on a
gurney, down an elevator that led to the parking
area located just outside of shock trauma's
ground-floor emergency room.

It was raining. Actually, it was more of a
consistent annoying drizzle. Nevertheless, the wet
roads would adversely affect the usually short
commute. Understandably adding to their travel
woes was the fact that it was the Friday before
Labor Day—when an impenetrable number of
automobiles transported their excited passengers
to their last blast of summer. They got exactly
what they expected. It took almost an hour to
travel the 15 minutes it should have taken.
Fortunately, they pulled into the driveway, at the
hospital, less than one minute before Jimmy
arrived.

The misty rain moistened Jimmy's face as he
was pulled out of the ambulance—safely secured to
his gurney. His transport team quickly rolled him
into the hospital, with his parents right behind
them, and went straight to the elevator. As they
took the elevator down to the brain trauma wing,

located on the lower level of the hospital's two floors, the driver of Jimmy's transport team was kicking himself, in the you know what, for taking the beltway. Regretfully, Joe and Lynn took the same route and they wholeheartedly shared in his frustration.

CHAPTER 11:   PRIMAL RECOVERY

Sherman Hospital's brain trauma wing was operating with a skeleton crew of medical care professionals, because it was the Labor Day weekend. If Joe and Lynn could have chosen a worse time to have their son transferred, they could not think of one. His very capable doctor was on-duty; but his rehabilitation team and social worker were on leave until Tuesday.

When Joe and Lynn arrived, on the day after Labor Day, Jimmy's social worker immediately approached them. She casually introduced herself and ungraciously exclaimed, "The 'Oh My God' portion of your son's unfortunate accident is over and it's time to focus on his rehabilitation. A team of state-certified specialists have already evaluated him, and they will be meeting with us later this afternoon to discuss their findings and outline a course of action." Joe and Lynn were somewhat floored by her demeanor, and apparently scripted approach, but they were very pleased with the fact that Jimmy was getting the attention he desperately needed.

They went to spend some quality time with their son. Lynn gave him all the Jimmy-addressed-cards that had been mailed to him. He quietly read each card, and sincerely reflected on the message each thoughtful well-wisher wanted to send him.

Joe taped the cards to the surrounding walls, as a constant reminder of the many caring people who wanted him to recover. Jimmy appreciatively smiled when he looked at all the cards.

Shortly thereafter, they met with his social worker and therapeutic team, as scheduled, and they ended up being more confused than comforted. His occupational therapist told them that she could not be sure about how much of a recovery they could expect in his right shoulder, arm, wrist, hand, and fingers. She said, "Unfortunately, he sustained a significant amount of peripheral nerve damage. When you combine that with his brain injury, I'm stuck with a lot of room for prognostic uncertainty." His physical therapist was equally uncertain about his final prognosis. He said, "My examination has ascertained that paralysis is not an issue, but it is too early to predict his final degree of recovery, because there are still too many unknowns." His speech therapist had a tendency to come across as being rather cold and assertive. She said, "My initial observation of his cognitive abilities clearly indicates that he is able to comprehend things at or near his age and grade level. Tomorrow, I will use an x-ray machine to determine his ability to swallow thin liquids. He will remain on nectar until he passes the test." The social worker redundantly summarized everything, and said, "After Jimmy is discharged, he will have to be monitored 24/7, by at least one of you, and he will have to be taught at home for the remainder of the 1st semester. A school-based team of professionals will assist you in making a decision for the 2nd semester. We will meet again in a couple of days to discuss his progress and establish a discharge date."

Joe and Lynn immediately went to see their son. His nurse was taking his vitals. She said, "His vital signs are all good. He's scheduled for therapy when I'm finished." So, they took "the walk" to take a break and talk. Joe curiously asked, "Do you have enough leave-time to stay with him for the rest of the 1st semester?" Lynn replied, "I may not have enough leave-time to keep visiting him while he's still in the hospital." It was at that moment when Joe believed that he understood one plausible reason for his son's miraculous survival. He would have to take the time off and try to take advantage of a unique opportunity to bond with Jimmy.

Joe and Lynn met with the triad of therapists and social worker, for the second time, on Thursday, September 7th. The therapists unanimously agreed on Friday, the 15th of September, as his projected discharge date. His social worker said, "I can assure you that they are rarely wrong in projecting a discharge date.

However, the final decision will ultimately have to be made by his doctor."

Joe and Lynn were very excited about the projected discharge date for two good reasons. Medical professionals believed that their son would be well enough to go home in a little over a week, and Lynn was quickly running out of leave-time. They were sincerely hoping and praying that Jimmy would live up to his therapists' expectations.

Jimmy's therapy sessions, on Friday, September 8th, went as well as each of his therapists had anticipated. His occupational therapist casually coerced him into getting dressed on his own, and aggressively made him do exercises to strengthen his "semi-paralyzed" right arm and hand. His physical therapist had him up on his feet and walking, with assistance, for the first time in almost a month. His speech therapist was subjecting him to painful shock treatments, in a somewhat sincere attempt, to get him ready to swallow thin liquids.

CHAPTER 12:   CHECKERS, CHESS, AND OLIVE OIL

Jimmy hated his hospital food diet. He willingly ingested their breakfast, because his parents weren't there and he wanted to appease his occupational therapist. However, after his parents arrived, he always insisted that they take care of his meals. They usually purchased their lunch in the hospital's cafeteria, and he consistently wanted them to bring him something to eat. He would only eat what they brought him, and that portion of the hospital meals in sealed containers—Boost pudding, sherbet, and ice cream. For dinner, his favorite meal was a burger, fries, and shake from Checkers. For dessert, he usually requested a McDonald's fruit and yogurt parfait.

Pre-accident Jimmy had nurtured an infatuated obsession with movies, and the local McDonald's had a Red Box video rental machine. Unfortunately, at the present time, he did not have a portable DVD player. Therefore, Joe thoughtfully decided to buy him one, and Jimmy was very excited when Joe gave it to him and told him about the Red Box at McDonald's. He very politely requested, "Please, go to the Red Box and phone me with the titles of the movies that are there." His parents excitedly complied, because they sincerely believed that they discovered a legitimate way to

leave him feeling content, each evening, when it
was time for them to go home.

Checkers was conveniently located in the
food court, of a nearby indoor shopping mall,
where Joe and Lynn usually ate their dinner. After
dinner, they would get in the line, at Checkers,
to order Jimmy's burger, fries, and shake. Joe
really did not mind bringing him something to eat,
but he was very concerned with the fact that his
son refused to eat the nutritional hospital food
his doctor had ordered.

His concern got him thinking. Then, out of
the blue, Joe decided to find a way to get Jimmy
to ingest olive oil. His reasoning was loosely
based on what he knew about "Lorenzo's Oil," from
a movie he had seen many years ago. He vaguely
remembered that the child depicted in the movie
had something wrong with his brain, and olive oil
was an essential ingredient in the final mixture
of chemicals that somehow worked to improve the
child's brain condition. Joe decided to approach
Jimmy's doctor and request his permission to let
Jimmy ingest olive oil. The puzzled physician
granted his request, and Joe immediately started
trying to get his son to dip bread in extra virgin
olive oil and eat it. Jimmy didn't like it—so, Joe
made a deal with him that would have made his
speech therapist grimace with despair. He said, "I
will give you almost any thin liquid of your

choice, if you will dip some bread in olive oil and eat it." Jimmy instantly agreed, but he had a difficult time fulfilling his part of the agreement. Consequentially, Joe tactfully restricted Jimmy's consumption of thin liquids, and concocted a devious plan to get as much olive oil into his diet as possible. He carefully opened Jimmy's burgers from Checkers and put extra virgin olive oil on the buns.

Without notice, a fourth therapist was plunged into Jimmy's formula for a speedy recovery. He was a young man, confined to an electric wheelchair, and Jimmy immediately seemed to like him. His official title was Recreational Therapist, and his initial approach was to entice Jimmy into playing a board game. The first game they played together was Yahtzee. As they played the game, he cleverly questioned Jimmy about his likes and dislikes. Jimmy replied, "I really like movies. My parents bought me a portable DVD player, so I could watch movies at night." Before Joe and Lynn left for the evening—a cart holding a 20" television and a DVD player was strategically placed in his room.

The sudden recreational approach to healing triggered Joe's curiosity, and the first thing he thought of was chess. At Jimmy's next recreational therapy session, Joe politely asked the therapist, "Do you have a chess set that I could borrow?" He

sullenly replied, "We do not have a chess set."
When the session ended, Joe and Lynn went to the
hospital gift shop and purchased an inexpensive
chess set, after which, they went to visit their
son in his room. Joe showed Jimmy the chess set
and cautiously asked, "Are you game?" Jimmy paused
for a brief moment and said, "Let's do it." Joe
was very concerned with the possibility that his
brain-injured son might be overwhelmed by a game
as challenging as chess, but he truly believed
that if he could get him playing chess and
consuming extra virgin olive oil, then he would be
helping him to heal. Lynn envisioned a legitimate
opportunity for some long over-due bonding,
between a father and son, that she wishfully hoped
would be carried-over into the time they would be
spending together after Jimmy was discharged. The
games began, and Joe rather convincingly beat his
son the first few times they played. Then, Joe
stopped using his queen and Jimmy began winning
more games than he lost. Father and son chess
matches became firmly implanted in the daily
routine—until English 11 and geometry
understandably replaced them, approximately one
month after their joyful inception.

CHAPTER 13:   THE PUTTING GREEN

It was during his second week's stay, at
Sherman Hospital, when Jimmy finally conceded to
letting his parents take him outside on pretty
days. They would take turns pushing him, in his
wheelchair, for several hundred yards through the
upper parking lot until they stopped to rest at a
picturesque pitching and putting green.

After taking a couple of breaths of outside
air, on their first excursion, Jimmy calmly
exclaimed—"It smells like the Grotto." He was
referring to the uniquely replicated "Grotto of
Lourdes" located at Mount Saint Mary's University
in Emmitsburg, Maryland. The Masdens regularly
prayed at the Grotto, every Christmas and Easter,
and their children went with them from the time
they were born. Jimmy always insisted on laying a
cross, made from a skinny stick and a defoliated
rhododendron leaf, on a statue of the baby Jesus,
lying in his manger, located near the exit. Joe
deceptively agreed with him—because, in his
opinion, not even an imaginary hint of the unique
flavor of the air at the Grotto would ever be
present on the grounds of Sherman Hospital.

On each occasion, after they arrived, Joe
walked out onto the artificial surface of the
putting green and said, "Jimmy, if you work hard
in therapy, then I can promise you that we will be

playing golf next summer." After which, he
casually pretended to putt an imaginary golf ball,
with an imaginary putter, into one of the several
real holes.

CHAPTER 14:   REUNITED

Less than a month after violently being struck by a two-ton SUV, Jimmy was healthy enough to be discharged. His therapists very diligently prepared his parents for every post-discharged scenario they could reasonably be expected to face.

In-between training sessions, they had to meet with Jimmy's social worker to finalize the outpatient arrangements. She said, "I can assure you that the transition from inpatient care to outpatient care, and homebound schooling, will take little or no effort on your part. I will take care of everything."

He was scheduled to be discharged at 1:00 PM, but the actual time depended on the delivery-time of the wheelchair, and walker, that had been ordered by his physical therapist. They went to see Jimmy, and his doctor was examining him to evaluate his readiness to be discharged. The extremely pleased physician happily discharged him, and left them with the vital instructions, and prescriptions, they would need to continue to keep their son's remarkable recovery moving in the right direction.

The mystical hour of the 1:00 PM discharge had come, and gone, and they were stuck waiting for the elusive "before you're discharged" medical equipment. Jimmy did not have any therapy sessions scheduled for the afternoon, so he decided to pass the time playing chess with his dad. Joe could easily sense his son's mounting anxiety as the minutes changed to hours. He knew that he was very anxious to get home—back to his own room, his own bed, and Zoso.

The medical equipment arrived at approximately 3:00 PM. Joe rushed to the delivery truck, hurriedly signed the paperwork and bolted to the parking lot to retrieve the car. He parked it at the entrance to the hospital and went in to ask his son's physical therapist for a favor. The physical therapist was cheerfully pushing Jimmy, in his new wheelchair, toward the hospital's front doors. Joe quickly approached him and asked him to stop. He pulled the puzzled physical therapist aside and said, "I promised Jimmy that he would leave here walking through the front doors. You have to help me keep my promise." They mutually agreed on a congenial compromise, and Jimmy walked through the front doors using his walker. His physical therapist was very pleased with his brazen decision to break the rules and assist Joe in making his promise a reality.

Their uneventful ride home was intensely infused with a special air of excitement—because, Jimmy was in the car and they were taking him home. Fortunately, they had just barely beaten the

rush hour traffic and the surprisingly pleasant
commute took less time than usual. Along the way
they stopped to get Jimmy's prescriptions filled,
and gas for the car. Shortly thereafter, Joe
pulled into the driveway that faced the front door
of the house they called home for a little more
than 20 years. Jimmy appeared to be nervous,
apprehensive, and excited. He anxiously gazed,
through the windshield, at the door that stood
between him and the little dog he longed to see
again. Through two pairs of loving parents' eyes—
it was truly a beautiful sight.

Joe insisted that Jimmy use his walker to
get from the car to the front door, and he
willingly complied. He barely struggled, as his
dad conscientiously adhered to the training that
he had carefully practiced under the watchful eye
of Jimmy's former physical therapist. The time had
come to open the front door and officially reunite
a boy with his dog. With the simple turn of a key,
an emotional moment was poised and ready to begin.
The door was opened and Jimmy cautiously entered
the house he chose to leave 22 days ago. A
courageous boy and his dog were happily reunited.
Zoso kept jumping up and down as he chased the
tennis balls that Joe had put on the rear legs of
Jimmy's walker.

Shortly after he went to his room, to retire
for the evening, Lynn phoned each of their parents

to share the good news. She cheerfully told them that Jimmy was finally back where he belonged, and they seemed to be elated. However, Lynn somehow sensed a lack of relief in their demeanor, and she was not at all surprised. She instinctively felt that their parents knew that the bumpy road ahead would be stressfully filled with an overabundance of challenging residual obstacles.

CHAPTER 15:   PATIENCE

On the following Monday, Lynn swiftly
shifted into high gear. She became a mother on a
mission. First, she secured an appointment with
Jimmy's pediatrician. Then, she called his school
to inquire about the arrangements that should have
been made to continue his education from home. The
school official replied, "I have the paperwork,
and it's all in order, but the earliest available
date for an IEP meeting is September 30." Lynn
cautioned him about the time her son had already
lost, and insisted, "You will have to come up with
a viable plan for making it up." He said, "I fully
understand the magnitude of the situation, and I
am very confident that we can mutually design and
implement an IEP that will effectively take care
of any lost time." He was apparently under the
impression that Jimmy was some kind of vegetable,
and Lynn was seriously wondering about how the
paperwork from Sherman Hospital may have misled
him. Then, she called Tulip Hill, a satellite of
Frederick Memorial Hospital, to secure
appointments for Jimmy's outpatient physical and
occupational therapy. The secretary said, "The
earliest I can schedule him for evaluations is the
middle of next week." Lynn replied, "Then, that
will have to do. Let's make the appointments."

In the meantime, Joe and Lynn took on the task of rehabilitating Jimmy, as best they could, on their own. They were determined to keep his muscles and peripheral nerves actively functioning. Joe focused on keeping him mobile. He took him shopping all over the city for a single-point cane, and to stores where he could drive their motorized shopping carts. He also took him out for lunch and a movie several times, and he frequently gave him reasons to go up to his room—so he could practice using the stairs. Lynn consistently made sure that he regularly took sit-down showers, washed his hands, and brushed his teeth—because she wanted him to establish a good hygienic routine. Joe was equally determined to keep the thinking part of his cerebral cortex challenged. In a very sincere effort to help him build some confidence and self-esteem—he humbly decided to let his son regularly, but not easily, beat him at chess.

Jimmy's pediatric appointment was with the same extraordinary woman that his parents had wisely chosen to care for each of their children from birth. When she opened the door to the examining room, she had the very same determined look in her eyes that Joe had witnessed, 16 years ago, when she was manually pumping air into Jimmy's tiny lungs. She thoroughly examined Jimmy and was amazed with his progress. She attentively listened to everything he had to say, and tried her best to reassure him. She said, "Your life-threatening injuries are far behind you, and it is going to take a lot of patience and determination, on your part, to complete the healing process." Unfortunately, her sensible words fell on the deaf ears of a teenager, who had astutely become accustomed to ingesting increasingly popular narcotic-based pain pills. The only thing Jimmy was interested in hearing was directly related to prescribed narcotics.

Medication had been a pressing issue with Jimmy throughout his ordeal, and it quickly turned into an almost unbearable dilemma. When he was in the hospital, the typical first course of action was to give him narcotic-based painkillers to keep him comfortable and quiet. Now, placed in the care of his long-time pediatrician, that option quickly vanished.

The doctor who treated him on one of his visits to the shock trauma clinic, while he was still a patient at Sherman Hospital, gave him 800mg of ibuprofen when he complained about the pain he was feeling. His doctor, at Sherman Hospital, openly criticized the shock trauma doctor's use of ibuprofen. He was concerned about the potential for an adverse side effect, because Jimmy was taking warfarin—a blood-thinning medication—and ibuprofen would thin his blood even more. He failed to mention the widely accepted fact that one 800mg dose, taken by a patient on warfarin, was medically considered to be quite safe. Nevertheless, Jimmy took it all in and decided that narcotic-based painkillers, which would not thin his blood, was his "no-brainer" course of action.

His beloved pediatrician was rather unfortunately handed the almost insurmountable task of convincing a 16-year-old male, recovering from a minor brain injury, that he could not take prescription narcotics for the rest of his life. She carefully studied the list of medications he was presently taking, cautiously decided to let him temporarily keep taking the oxycodone, and added a couple that she sincerely believed would be beneficial.

Perhaps, the largest obstacle medical professionals have to overcome, when prescribing medicine, is the brutal fact that different people often respond differently to the same medications. Therefore, finding the right combination of prescription drugs is governed by the auspices of trial and error, which takes time and patience. That fact undoubtedly became the most difficult problem Joe and Lynn had to face, as parents, for quite some time to come. They could only thank God that Jimmy's doctors, and pharmacists, were with them every step of the way.

CHAPTER 16:   ROUND TWO

On Monday, the 25th of September, Jimmy started his second round of physical and occupational therapy with his newly appointed therapists. After evaluating him, they mutually recommended four one-hour sessions of both therapies, each week, until his next evaluation in about a month.

His physical therapist could not do much more than stretch him, because of the involuntary clonic spasms in his right leg. Therefore, he recommended that Jimmy be fitted with a leg brace, with a custom-made insole, specifically designed to alleviate the pressure-point stimuli that were apparently triggering the clonic spasms. Jimmy had to have the leg brace before he could even attempt to begin the aggressive level of physical therapy that he needed. He also, rather convincingly, quickly talked him into retiring his walker and using his single-point cane. Less than two weeks later, after he was properly fitted with his leg brace, his single-point cane joined the retired walker.

Jimmy's experience, with his occupational therapist, was like riding a roller coaster. At the onset, all she could do was stretch his right shoulder and begin to work on helping him redevelop his fine motor skills. Jimmy consistently worked hard to gain remarkable improvements in his ability to use his right arm and hand for more than a month. Then, something caused him to change—he suddenly decided to fake a bizarre shoulder spasm at the beginning of his weight-bearing therapy sessions. He made it appear as if any form of weight-bearing therapy would trigger a tremor, and that day's session ended early. On the last occasion, Joe inquisitively said, "I know you're doing it on purpose. Please, tell me why." Jimmy sharply answered, "I don't need that kind of therapy." Joe asked, "What kind of therapy do you need?" Jimmy replied, "The kind a good doctor is willing to prescribe."

The IEP meeting was held, as scheduled, on the 28th of September. The meeting began with the usual introductions, and ended when Joe insisted, "Jimmy will never be labeled as an exceptional student." The very capable educator in charge was somewhat shocked with Joe's claim, because he was well aware of the fact that Jimmy had sustained a traumatic brain injury. Joe said, "Jimmy should be tested by your speech therapist before we address his status. We just need to focus on writing a 504 plan to adequately cover any temporary exceptional needs." The IEP meeting was adjourned with the stipulation that Jimmy be tested by their speech therapist. A 504 meeting was then quickly convened, because the educator in charge of IEP

meetings was also in charge of 504 meetings. It
was unanimously agreed upon that Jimmy be placed
in their homebound program for the first semester,
and a somewhat liberal 504 plan was designed to
address any minor disabilities that he may have to
overcome to be successful.

His parents were very pleased with the
selection of homebound teachers. His English
teacher, who had a strong background in music,
tactfully managed to get him interested in
learning how to play a guitar, as she skillfully
attempted to coax him into enjoying reading and
analyzing classical literature. His geometry
teacher also caringly encouraged him to pursue his
newfound interest in guitar, as she tried to teach
him how to understand and respect the
uncompromising methodology of proving that various
angles and line segments somehow made the world go
round.

Suddenly, it was the first week in October—
slightly less than 40 days after the second
feather. Jimmy was tolerating physical and
occupational therapy; making progress in English
and geometry; and anxiously waiting to hear from
his speech therapist. He had an appointment, on
the 4th of October, with his team of doctors at
shock trauma. It was imperative for Joe and Lynn
to give his regularly scheduled follow-up visits
at shock trauma a priority status, because they

were cautiously monitoring his dissected carotid artery.

He had to have a blood test, to evaluate kidney function, before they could administer the dye that was needed to obtain a reliable comparative CT scan visual of the hopefully healing artery. After the results were ready, they fortunately met with the doctor in charge of the shock trauma unit who admitted Jimmy on the night of his accident. The news was good. He said, "The artery appears to be healing, as we expected, and we are still very optimistic about continuing to let it heal on its own." Joe asked, "Can Jimmy visit with some of his friends, and take a trip New York—to visit his grandfather and go to his brother's homecoming football game?" His rather unique reply will probably stay with Joe forever. He simply stated, "You can't just put him on a couch wrapped-up in bubble wrap. Yes, he can visit with his friends and go to his brother's football game—it would probably do him some good."

Jimmy's mental capacity was thoroughly tested by a speech therapist, on October 11th, and the preliminary results were very encouraging. On Friday, the 20th of October, they traveled to New York to visit with Joe's father and go to Jack's homecoming football game. The game was played on a sunny Saturday afternoon; and they fortunately witnessed a rather lop-sided home-team victory in

which an under-sized Jack, only a sophomore, got
his first chance to play in a college football
game. His coach put him in, as a member of the
punt-team, on what would be the last play of the
game. An errant punt attempt was blocked and the
game ended. Unfortunately, Jack did not get a
chance to show them what he could do, but he did
get the chance to show his parents what kind of
coaching staff they had at Iona College, and they
were very pleased.

A second IEP meeting was convened on
November 2nd, and Joe's earlier belief related to
labeling him as an exceptional student was
confirmed. His scores ranged from average to well-
above average on the battery of tests administered
by his speech therapist. Based on the test
results, he did not qualify for exceptional
student status. Therefore, they mutually agreed to
keep him on his 504 plan and meet again, in
January, just before it was time for him to return
to school.

Closer to home, another staff of genuinely
good-hearted people went out of their way to make
Joe and Lynn feel special. Jimmy had to have his
blood tested, twice a week, to regulate his
consumption of warfarin, and Tulip Hill's
unforgettable staff consistently treated them like
royalty.

CHAPTER 17: NO END IN SIGHT

Every new beginning emerges at a prior beginning's end. On October 26th, Jimmy ended his occupational therapy sessions, and his physical therapy sessions were more than adequately reduced to three times each week. His parents took him to see his doctor at Sherman hospital, for the last time, on October 30th. His very thorough examination left them happily pondering his one word description of their son's progress— "Remarkable!"

His next appointment with the team of doctors at shock trauma, who were anxiously monitoring his carotid artery injury, was on November 21st. The optimistic prognosis was very encouraging, as the serious injury still appeared to be healing—but, another necessary monitory appointment was scheduled for January 11th. They left feeling hopeful that it would mark the end of their visits to shock trauma, because Joe was scheduled to go "back to teaching" on January 15th and Jimmy was scheduled to go "back to school" exactly one week later.

Homebound schooling was going extremely well. Jimmy genuinely liked both of his teachers and he very willingly did everything they expected of him. They did not show him any pity, or act as if they felt sorry for him. They quietly displayed

some respect and understanding for the unique
circumstances that had brought them together, and
he uncharacteristically reciprocated. With his
dad's help, and the guidance of two very gracious
teachers, the "should have probably gotten C's"
student generously received A's in English and
geometry for the first semester.

Jimmy's physical therapist requested a
meeting, on January 4th, to tell Joe that he could
not do anything else for him while he was still
experiencing the clonic spasms in his right leg.
He was running, jumping, skipping, hopping, and
sidestepping—as he long as he was wearing his leg-
brace. His physical therapist said, "He is not
ready to be discharged. If you can find a way to
get his leg muscles injected with botox, then he
can resume his therapy." Jimmy agreed to getting
the botox injections, and an appointment with a
physical medicine specialist at Children's
Hospital in Washington, D.C. was rather quickly
secured. However, he woefully would not get the
opportunity to address the problem—because the CT
angiogram taken at shock trauma, on January 11th,
revealed that his carotid artery injury was not
100% healed. The shock trauma doctors, driven by
professional logic, refused to settle for less.
Therefore, he had to stay on the warfarin and
could not be injected with botox. They were forced
to schedule another mandatory appointment, to get

another CT angiogram taken, on March 14th. They could only wait and hope that it would be the final one.

CHAPTER 18:   A NEW FORM OF THERAPY

    Shortly after Jimmy had nephariously decided
to end his occupational therapy sessions, back in
October, Lynn tactfully talked him into visiting
with a friendly couple who owned the local music
store. She curiously felt compelled to support his
recently acquired desire to learn how to play the
guitar, by purchasing him one of his own. Joe was
understandably convinced that, because Jimmy
refused to go to occupational therapy, he needed
something to take its place. He reasoned that
learning how to play the guitar would
therapeutically improve his son's eye/hand
coordination and give his brain a strenuous
challenging workout at the same time. The elated
proprietors of the music store generously gave
Jimmy an Ibanez steel string acoustic guitar for
free. Lynn purchased a stand for it, and his
parents left feeling queasily hopeful that they
might be pointing a confused, nervous teenager in
the right direction.

    Jimmy excitedly asked his homebound geometry
teacher to teach him how to play something on his
new guitar, but she never got around to honoring
his benign request. On the other hand, his
homebound English teacher casually mentioned that
she was taking her son to the local music store,
for guitar lessons, and she was very pleased with

the results. That got Joe's wheels turning; but, rather than asking Jimmy to consider taking guitar lessons at the music store—he began to devise a plan that might motivate him into seriously taking it into consideration.

First, he took him to Sam's Club and intentionally walked slowly down the aisle that displayed a variety of musical instruments. He was hoping that his son would want to stop and take a closer hands-on look at the guitars, and he got his wish. Jimmy took an inexpensive Fender Stratocaster replica, marketed as a Fender Starcaster, from its stand on the shelf and attempted to play it. Joe politely asked, "Do you want to learn how to play an electric guitar?" Jimmy instantly replied, "Yes, I think I do." Joe asked, "Would you really try to learn how to play it if I bought it for you?" Jimmy said, "Yes." Feeling confident that he had successfully initiated the first part of his plan, Joe purchased the Fender Starcaster package, with a big smile on his face, and they went straight home.

Joe slyly speculated that his son would have a difficult time using the "How to Play the Guitar" DVD that was conveniently included in the package, so he intentionally encouraged him to try it. Jimmy willingly cooperated, and he was, as Joe had envisioned, frustrated and bored with the

pedagogy utilized by the DVD's guitar teacher.
Jimmy said, "I want to learn how to play songs
that I like. I don't care about the notes, cords,
and juvenile songs on the DVD." Joe used the
expected reaction as an opportunity to initiate
the second part of his plan. He said, "I
completely understand where you are coming from."
Then, he boldly asked, "Are you willing to take
guitar lessons at the music store?" Jimmy
vehemently responded with a resounding "No!" Joe
had duly anticipated the negative response and
calmly moved on to phase three. He immediately
suggested, "Let's watch one of your Jimi Hendrix
videos." While they were watching Hendrix wail
away at Woodstock, Joe said, "I think we should
watch all of your 1960's and 70's rock videos
whenever we have some free time in the afternoon."

Over the next few weeks, they watched videos
made by Jimi Hendrix, The Beatles, John Lennon,
and The Doors. Joe tactfully interacted with him
while they were watching, and he rather quickly
determined that Jimmy undeniably seemed to possess
an unrelenting respect for the outstanding guitar-
playing ability Hendrix was blessed with, and he
decided to use it to formulate another plan—
specifically designed to motivate him into taking
guitar lessons at the music store. Joe surmised
that, if he purchased a real Fender Stratocaster
that closely resembled the one Hendrix played at

Woodstock, then he could effectively bribe his son into taking guitar lessons. He purchased a "Made in Mexico" white Fender Stratocaster for $399.99, which he really could not afford, and gave it to Jimmy as one of his Christmas presents. He was genuinely surprised, and joyfully expressed his satisfaction; but, he still refused to take the guitar lessons.

Jimmy kept breaking strings on his new guitar, which resulted in his dad's frequent deployment to the music store to purchase replacements. On one of his, "I'm really not a fixture" guitar-string-purchasing-trips Joe casually mentioned the guitar lesson dilemma to one of the store's co-owners. She immediately, and conscientiously, suggested that he tell Jimmy that he could take a one-half hour lesson for $20.00, without any further obligation, and she would waive the fee if he did not want to continue. Joe went home, replaced Jimmy's broken guitar string for the umpteenth time, and prudently told him about the co-owner's generous offer. Jimmy paused, to think about it for a moment, and curiously replied, "OK, I'll try it. When do you want to take me?" Joe quickly answered, "How does tomorrow sound?." Jimmy smiled and said, "It sounds like we're going."

CHAPTER 19:   MAKING HEADWAY

The very next day, Jimmy carried his beloved Stratocaster, safely secured in its soft-sided gig bag, into the music store to take his trial guitar lesson. When the lesson was over, he casually emerged sporting a huge grin and an unanticipated swagger. Joe asked him if he wanted to continue taking guitar lessons, and he could easily sense a bit of sarcastic excitement in his, "What do you think?" reply. They mutually established a weekly guitar lesson day and time, and Joe victoriously wrote a check to pay for the first month's lessons. As they were exiting the store, Jimmy promised, "Dad, I will be playing Jimi Hendrix's version of "The Star Spangled Banner" at Woodsville High School's homecoming football game in the fall." Joe was intrigued with his son's newfound confidence and conviction, smart enough to know that it would never happen, and illogically encouraged him to pursue his unreasonable goal.

Jimmy successfully managed to master the beginning of Hendrix's "Star Spangled Banner" by the end of his first real guitar lesson, and he continued to make strides in future lessons. Then, he became frustrated with the blaring rockets and bursting bombs guitar rifts Hendrix had invented, and perfected, and he wanted to give up. His

guitar teacher successfully motivated him saying,
"You would need Hendrix's stack of Marshall amps,
and wah pedal, to even come close to recreating
those rifts." Jimmy decided to temporarily put the
rifts on hold, and simply choose another song to
learn, because he was having fun.

Jimmy and Joe were forced to continue their
education at home for the first semester of the
school year, and the time was quickly approaching
when they were both expected to return to their
respective schools for the second semester.
Unfortunately, the schools were in different
states, and were operating on different schedules.
Joe was supposed to report one week earlier than
Jimmy, but Jimmy's homebound schooling was going
to end a week later and a parent had to be there.
Joe appropriately notified his principal, well in
advance of the obvious discrepancy, and she
instantly granted him the additional leave-time.
Joe graciously thanked her, and conscientiously
informed her that he was confident that he would
report to work on the following Monday. Her
carefully worded reply made him feel like it was
not soon enough, but he really did not have any
choice in the matter.

On the day before his return to school, Joe
was busy making preparations, when Jimmy walked
into the kitchen to take his medicine. Joe wanted
to give his son a hug and tell him that he loved

him, but "something" stopped him. Less than an hour later, Lynn informed Joe that both school systems were closed because of the snow that was falling. Jimmy and Joe were curiously granted a second last day to spend together. Joe wanted to believe, in his heart, that the snow day resulted from the fact that he had not said "see-you-later" to his son at that point in time. He spent the unexpected snow day shoveling snow, playing chess with Jimmy, and mentally preparing himself for his possible return to school on the following day.

The following day's weather was forecasted to be impeccable, and a rather intriguing interaction between a father and son astounded Lynn. Joe sensibly realized, from the weather report, that he and Jimmy would probably be going to school in the morning and he nervously pondered saying "see-you-later," when the day-old scenario coincidentally re-established itself. Joe and Lynn were sitting at their computers when Jimmy walked into the kitchen to take his medicine. Joe quickly followed him into the kitchen and said, "We're going back to school tomorrow." Then, he opened his arms to give his son a hug, and Jimmy very willingly hugged his father. While they were engaged in the rare embrace, Lynn clearly heard Joe say, "I love you Jimmy." A barely audible reply brought Lynn to tears when Jimmy softly whispered, "I love you, too."

CHAPTER 20: MOVING FORWARD

From the moment they walked through the all-too-familiar revolving front doors which granted them access to the shock trauma clinic, and radiology department, the walls in the building seemed to be exuding an invigorating form of aromatherapy that pleasantly permeated the air with the intoxicating flavor of confidence.

Jimmy endured another CT angiogram, and his parents survived another lunch in their cafeteria. His 1:00 PM appointment with the Team B doctor on call was surprisingly kept on time, but with an unusual twist. The doctor anxiously entered the examination room, briefly questioned Joe and Lynn, and half-heartedly examined Jimmy as if he was stalling. Then, he politely excused himself on the premise that he was going to view the results of Jimmy's CT angiogram.

Joe was the first to recognize that something unusual was happening. Shortly after the Team B doctor left, he said, "Lynn, Jimmy's primary physician is in the room across the hall, and he appears to be focusing on a computer monitor." Less than a minute later, the esteemed doctor casually walked into the examination room. An unusually large contingent of five medical professionals attempted to file in behind him. He calmly took a seat on a stool, while his contingent of followers crowded the outer entrance of the room; two of which had no other choice but to uncomfortably view the proceedings from the hallway—standing on tip-toe and straining their necks. He quietly examined Jimmy, and asked the Team B doctor, "What did the CT angiogram reveal?" His reply will forever echo a complacent remembrance of what they had hoped to hear that fateful day—"He's 100% healed." Without hesitation, the primary physician officially released him from their care, and cautiously warned his parents, "You will still have many "residuals" to overcome." Perennially the pessimist at times like this, Joe firmly believed that the satisfactory end to one problem meant that the beginning of a new one was probably right around the corner. He immediately began to worry about what the good doctor meant by "residuals."

Walking out of shock trauma, for the final time, was quite emotional—to say the least. The team of doctors congenially asked Joe and Lynn to call them if there was anything they could do for them, and they very politely requested that they visit whenever they could. The nurse, who had been there from the beginning of their ordeal, cheerfully hugged each of them and insisted that they stay in touch. Joe and Lynn will never forget them, but they had too many residual "fish to fry" before they could even attempt to initiate and plan a cordial visit that would be convenient for everyone.

Moving forward, Lynn expeditiously contacted the physical medicine specialist at Children's Hospital in D.C., and successfully secured an appointment to have Jimmy's right leg muscles injected with botox—exactly one week later. Joe envisioned the upcoming appointment as a testimony to support his belief that the treatment at shock trauma really did not end; it was just being replaced by the, more than likely, multiple treatments Jimmy would be receiving at Children's.

On the appointed day, the first day of spring, Jimmy insisted that they drive to D.C. for his botox treatment and Joe begrudgingly complied. Joe fully expected a tumultuous journey—but, on that particular day, the commute on I-270 was not nearly as bad as he had anticipated. However, he found out later that they were very fortunate to have been traveling just minutes ahead of an apparent "road-rage" incident that left two people dead. The evening news reported that the authorities had not located the driver of the vehicle, who allegedly caused the accident, but a dog that was traveling with the victims was amazingly found unharmed.

The semi-paralyzing botox was successfully injected into some of Jimmy's right leg muscles, but an unanticipated problem reared its ugly head in the recovery room. Jimmy constantly complained, to his nurse, about the pain he was feeling. It escalated to a point when his parents urgently had to do something to stop his nurse from injecting him with morphine. In a hastily convened behind closed doors meeting, with his doctor and nurse, Lynn openly revealed, "I believe that Jimmy is becoming addicted to narcotic pain medication. His pediatrician shares my belief and does not want him taking any narcotic-based drugs." His doctor wisely decided to take charge of the situation. He thoughtfully questioned Jimmy about every pain he was feeling, and Jimmy quickly motioned to the lower right side of his back. The tactful doctor logistically prescribed a Lidoderm patch that could easily be positioned anywhere on his back where he was experiencing pain. However disappointed, as he may have been, he had no choice but to accept his doctor's skillfully recommended solution to his seemingly never-ending enigma with narcotic pain medication. At least, for the time being, the problem was apparently solved. Jimmy regularly requested the Lidoderm patch for a week or two, and then only sporadically after that—because the pain mysteriously migrated from his back to his head. The closer it came to his follow-up appointment, the faster the pain migrated to his head.

An imperative follow-up visit had reasonably been scheduled for May 15th, and Joe anxiously decided to drive. The 10:30 AM appointment suitably placed them in a win-win morning commute time, and they literally cruised down I-270 to the inner-loop of the Washington beltway. After which, they effortlessly traveled south on Georgia Avenue to the double left turn, on and off of Michigan Avenue, that quickly brought them to the hospital's, under-reconstruction, parking garage. Nevertheless, they later learned that they just beat another road rage incident that left an off-duty policewoman fighting for her life in shock trauma. They fortunately located a convenient place to park, and checked-in with the Neurology Department's receptionist with plenty of time to spare.

The physical medicine specialist was extremely pleased with the results of Jimmy's botox treatment, and was about to schedule his next appointment—when Jimmy complained about feeling an unmanageable amount of weakness in his right leg. After observing him walking, the doctor recommended that he resume, in the very least, a limited regimen of physical therapy. The logical recommendation was instantly rejected by Jimmy's stubborn attempt to use his doctor's suggestion as a means for obtaining a prescription painkiller—when he said, "I will only go back to therapy, if

I could take a pain-pill before each session."
Each of them wisely decided that silence was the
best reply.

Joe was feeling rather fortunate as they
left the parking garage with plenty of time to
make it back to Frederick, and the familiar Taco
Bell where Jimmy wanted to have lunch—the very
same Taco Bell where he had lunch with his son,
almost every Thursday, for the past seven months.

CHAPTER 21: JIMMY TO JIMI

Jimmy's guitar teacher wisely decided to teach him how to read tablatures, instead of standard notes, and he loved it. Over the next few months of half-hour Thursdays—he started learning Clapton's "Wonderful Tonight," Lennon's "Imagine," and also managed to finish Hendrix's "Star Spangled Banner"—minus the blaring rockets and bursting bombs. Joe was extremely pleased with what was happening, and suggested, "Jimmy, I truly believe that you could find a way to modify Hendrix's "Star Spangled Banner" into your own version." After a few more lessons that incorporated the use of a dad-gifted Cry Baby wah pedal, and the opportunity to think about it for a while—Jimmy surprisingly decided to agree with his dad. Then, it occurred to Joe that the guitar lessons had both arms and hands working full-time with his brain—and, he had unintentionally incorporated Jimmy's left leg and foot with the addition of the wah pedal.

Quite pleased with himself, Joe thoughtfully decided to take that challenging addition to the next level. He purchased a Digitech Artist's Series foot pedal that already had the effects for seven popular Jimi Hendrix tunes digitally programmed into it, which included the "Star Spangled Banner." Joe called it an early birthday present, because he made the impromptu purchase a couple of weeks before his son's 17th birthday.

Jimmy took his guitar lessons very seriously, as he was frequently heard practicing when he should have been studying. Joe and Lynn really did not mind, because he considered their asking him about schoolwork as meddling. All they could do was show him that they trusted him, and be happy that he was developing a strong interest in something that had the amazing potential to be a very beneficial part of his still-pending complete recovery.

One of the rather obscure songs he had started to learn, "A Tear for Eddie," written by Ween—an alternative rock group from Pennsylvania— was replaced by Hendrix's "The Wind Cries Mary," after he secured the Digitech Artist's Series foot pedal. However, Lynn had something up her sleeve that would boost every stride that had been made, and take Jimmy's guitar playing therapy to a level that Joe could have never imagined. Lynn had received a very low fixed-rate credit card offer in the mail and uncharacteristically decided to apply for it. She was almost instantly approved and the card was quickly issued.

Several weeks before his 17th birthday, Jimmy started talking about getting a job to get the money he needed to buy a guitar that he wanted. Joe adeptly questioned him about the guitar's

brand, model, and finish. After which, he openly
shared his son's detailed responses with Lynn.
Jimmy clearly described a Gibson Les Paul Classic—
with a 1960's neck and a Vintage Sunburst finish.
With nothing but love, and a newly issued credit
card, mom granted his wish.

The guitar was scheduled to be delivered on
Jimmy's 17th birthday. Joe decided to take the day
off, so he could be there. He spent most of the
day closely monitoring the front of his house for
the UPS delivery van. The anxiously anticipated
arrival occurred around 2:00 PM. Joe alertly
called to Jimmy, who was upstairs in his room,
"Hey Jimmy, I need you to answer the door." A
rather curious son obeyed his father's mundane
request and arrived at the front door just seconds
before the UPS man was poised to knock. He quickly
opened the door, and the expression on his face
was no less than priceless when he saw the word
Gibson written in large letters on the box being
delivered. He politely signed for the delivery,
carefully carried the box into the house, and
hosting eyes as big as silver dollars, curiously
asked his dad, "What's this all about?" Joe
casually said, "You'll have to ask your mom."
Then, he happily helped his son open the box, and
Jimmy's eyes grew to super-sized silver dollars
when he saw a genuine Gibson Les Paul Classic
guitar, snuggly secured in the white lining of its

hard-shell case, staring back at him—yearning for his love and affection, and begging to be played.

Jimmy swaggered into his next guitar lesson proudly toting his new guitar, because he was anxious to learn the rest of "A Tear for Eddie." His post Digitech foot pedal loss of interest was rekindled after he had the opportunity to play some of it on his new Les Paul. His guitar teacher was very agreeable, and he almost finished learning the song.

After his lesson, he got into the car saying, "I'm close to finishing "A Tear for Eddie," and I want to start learning some Led Zeppelin songs." Joe asked, "Did you know that I went to a Led Zeppelin concert, on Valentine's Day, back in 1975?" Jimmy answered, "No, but wow, that must have been awesome." Joe very simply replied, "Yes, yes it was."

CHAPTER 22:   ALMOST ONE YEAR LATER

The summer was, yet again, another rollercoaster ride of extreme highs and lows. When the school year ended, Jimmy's final grades for the second semester were still unknown. His guidance counselor told Lynn, "I have kept in touch with his teachers, and they said he's passing and his behavior in class has been extraordinary. It's almost as if he was a different person, and his teachers are dumbfounded." Lynn shared the news with Joe, and that enlightening bit of information brought him back to his childhood—when his mother had caringly advised him saying, "Joe, I don't care about grades as long as you do your best and respect your teachers. The way you present yourself directly reflects on the type of family you come from, and family is everything. Your father and I taught you manners—and, when you're a grown man, I know you will be successful if you use them." Then, he smiled and thought to himself, "Where there's a will—there's a way."

Jimmy was still an outpatient at Children's Hospital, in D.C., where he was rather infrequently being seen by the physical medicine specialist who consistently recommended that he resume a regimen of physical therapy. Jimmy steadfastly refused, so his doctor referred him to

a local neurologist-turned-therapist with the hope
that he could somehow change his mind. The newly
acquired therapist was also expected to address
some serious anger-management issues that
threatened to destroy the very fiber upon which
his loving family's relationships had been built,
and assist with his senior year transition back to
school at the same time.

Jimmy and his parents met with him on June
20th, and they were scheduled to see him again on
July 6th. It was too early to speculate on his
willingness to accept the upcoming diagnosis and
proposed treatment; or the potential benefits his
parents sincerely hoped to see generated by their
stringent attempt to keep him congenially
committed to following his new therapist's pending
professional advice. They very patiently had to
wait to get their answers.

Joe took Jimmy to a local driving range,
shortly after their meeting with the therapist,
and he surprisingly showed his dad that he could
still swing a golf club. He could not hit the ball
as far as he used to, but he somehow managed to
put the face of the club somewhere on the ball and
propel it in a forward direction. Joe was elated.
He began to visualize himself playing golf with
his son—as he reminisced about the times, at
Sherman Hospital's putting green, when he had
promised him that it would happen. After they

finished hacking ball after ball, Joe said, "I think we both need a few more trips here before we'll be ready to play on a golf course." Jimmy replied, "I think you're right."

The 24th of June was the day before Lynn's 50th birthday, ten days before her and Joe's 30th wedding anniversary, and 302 stressful days after their youngest child's nearly fatal encounter with a Chevy Blazer. It was a picturesque day, so they took him to a nearby state park and rented a rowboat to take him fishing on their pristine lake. He got a lot of nibbles—but, he ended up empty-handed, angry, and very disappointed. He furiously carried his frustration, later that evening, into Lynn's birthday dinner at Firestone's Restaurant in downtown Frederick. A very special occasion quickly descended into an incontrovertible fiasco. It began when Joe could not find a parking space close enough to the restaurant to suit Jimmy, and it ended with Joe never wanting to go there again. Joe was still suffering with indigestion, two days later, when he nervously reported for his annual physical exam. Lynn tried her best to relax him saying, "Joe, I can't blame Jimmy, and I forgive him. I can't even begin to comprehend every latent pain he is feeling, but I feel certain that he's battling with PTSD."

The vast majority of Jimmy's outbursts were always directly related to his medication, and Joe began to believe that his current friends might be influencing him into thinking that he was taking the wrong medicine. Joe was not sure that his friends were misleading him, because every one of his medicinal complaints had been consistently verified, by his doctor, as potential side effects. Joe and Lynn were securely stuck between that rock and a hard place again, and they sincerely did not know where to turn. They could only hope that the July 6th appointment, with the certified therapist, would somehow end with an agreeable cocktail of prescription medications that would swiftly take him to a point in time when he would want to wean off all of them.

Their sincere hopes inexplicably vanished when Jimmy boldly refused to cooperate with the therapist. They ended up having to take him to the emergency room, to procure a temporarily prescribed sedative, just to make it through the next few days. The general consensus was that he was probably battling with some form of post-traumatic stress disorder, and an appointment was quickly scheduled with a new neurologist, conveniently located in Rockville, MD, for Thursday, July 26th.

After their second outing to the driving range, on Monday, July 9th, Joe was too anxious to

play a game of golf with his son to wait any
longer. In the early afternoon of the following
day, they played the first nine holes on Maple Run
Golf Course, in Thurmont, MD—a public course that
President Clinton frequented when he was staying
at Camp David. They took turns playing the same
ball, Jimmy drove the cart like a pro, and they
both had a great time. Joe could hardly wait to do
it again, so he asked, "Would you like to play the
back nine tomorrow?" Jimmy thought about it for a
moment, and then suggested, "I think we should
spend some more time at the driving range." Joe
casually replied, "I think you may be right. Let's
go to the driving range tomorrow, and play the
back nine on Thursday." Jimmy answered, "That
sounds like a plan to me." Over the next two
weeks, they contently flip-flopped practice and
playing time between the driving range and the
golf course. Perhaps, more importantly, they were
bonding as a father and son.

On July 26, Jimmy kept his appointment with
the neurologist in Rockville. He thoroughly
examined him and said, "I am confident that I
could successfully take control of your
medications and the botox injections." Jimmy and
his parents anxiously agreed to accept his offer.
That meant that they could stop taking the much
longer commute to D.C., and considering the fact
that their last two D.C. road trips revolved

around two very serious incidents of road rage—neither of them was relishing the thought of a third.

The apparently successful appointment perplexed them, because he put Jimmy on a new medication and it seemed to be working. There were no angry outbursts or complaints, and his demeanor and attitude were much improved. For a relatively brief period, he was not the same headstrong, defiant boy that he had been for the past few months.

Then, on Tuesday, August 7th, things dramatically took a turn for the worse. Jimmy woke up much earlier than usual, and informed his dad that he was going to hangout with the two guys he was with on the night of the accident—because he had not seen them all summer. Joe was very concerned, but there was nothing he could do to stop him. He had every good reason to be worried, because the pre-July 26th Jimmy suddenly reemerged later that evening. Almost as quickly as they appeared to have ended, his spoiled-kid tantrums, directly related to prescription medication, mysteriously returned—but the duration period was somewhat shorter. Lynn contacted the neurologist, as soon as she could, and he suggested that she give him a smaller dose of his evening medicine each morning. Jimmy instantly agreed with his doctor's recommendation, but Joe was inherently skeptical. It was very difficult for him to comprehend that the solution to dealing with a teenager's growing obsession with prescribed medication was to prescribe more.

Throughout the summer, Jimmy continued to take his guitar lessons very seriously. At one point, back in mid-July, he casually told his dad, "When I'm playing my guitar I lose all track of time." By summer's end, he was learning how to play Hendrix's "Electric Ladyland" instrumental and he was looking forward to tackling Led Zeppelin's "Stairway to Heaven" in the very near future. Joe wanted to believe that—somehow, someday, the guitar would replace his son's apparent infatuation with highly addictive prescription drugs.

CHAPTER 23: WHAT MIRACLE?

A miracle, as defined by Webster's New
Compact Format Dictionary, is "a wonder, a
prodigy, and a supernatural event." Rather
surprisingly, to his parents at least, Webster
left out the one word that Jimmy's doctor at
Sherman Hospital had used to describe his
progress—"remarkable." Webster defines remarkable
as "noteworthy, unusual, strange, or
distinguished." There seems to be a fine line
between the two definitions. Could it be that one
was meant to be used by the church and the other
by the state? To almost every outsider, Joe and
Lynn have undoubtedly managed to approach full
circle in the miracle department—or have they?

In at least the past 25 years, every single
one of the many pedestrians, struck by vehicles on
MD 176, was instantly killed. Joe and Lynn did not
know about the eye-witnessed mystical light that
apparently brought their son back from the dead,
or the accompanying iridescent feather, but they
knew in their hearts that it was a bona fide
miracle. At the present time, they were still very
emotionally dazed and confused. Perhaps, Joe had
forgotten about the similar circumstances that
accompanied Jimmy's miraculous, and remarkable,
birth. Nevertheless, he compassionately felt as if
he would be lost without his son and he refused to

give up. He just wanted to take him golfing and use that valuable time to help guide him in a reasonably sensible direction.

Joe frequently reminisced about a poem his mother asked him to read, and take with him, when he went away to college. It helped him to relax when Jimmy was "unintentionally" giving him a hard time—a rather common trait in patients recovering from a traumatic brain injury.

Don't Quit

When things go wrong as they sometimes will,
And the road you're trudging seems all uphill,
When the funds are low, and the debts are high,
And you want to smile, but you have to sigh,
When care is pressing you down a bit,
Rest if you must, but don't you quit.

Life is queer with its twists and turns,
As everyone of us sometimes learns,
And many a failure turns about,
When he might have won had he stuck it out.
Don't give up though the pace seems slow,
You may succeed with another blow.

Success is failure turned inside out,
The silver tint of the clouds of doubt,
And you never can tell just how close you are,
It may be near when it seems so far,
So stick to the fight when you're hardest hit,
It's when things seem worse,
That you must not quit.

Author Unknown

There was little doubt in his parents' minds that divine intervention kept Jimmy alive, when his battered body came to rest on the consistently fatal material that MD 176 was paved with. The only thing that naggingly puzzled them was—"Why?" Was it the fact that Joe, instead of Lynn, was synergistically forced into taking a full semester of the school year off to care for him? After all, it was during that very unusual period when a father and son truly bonded for the first time. Joe momentarily considered believing that Jimmy needed significantly more than a "kick in the butt" to effectively turn his life around, but he curiously envisioned that it happened for a reason yet to be revealed. Lynn was happily content with the fact that she would always remember what is, and what should probably never be.

Their latest analysis, of the obvious conundrum, directly pointed to love as the most logical answer. Joe's unconditional love for Jimmy was permanently changed when he truly felt like he was going to lose him. It was transformed into an enduring love that will surely be tested and undoubtedly pass the test of time. They reasonably considered the love they earnestly felt from the difficult to estimate number of people who prayed for Jimmy all over the world. It most certainly helped to give them the unrelenting determination, the mountain of faith, the tons of hope, and the endless supply of love they needed to keep their dream alive.

A rather interesting story, directly related to the extent at which the news of Jimmy's "near-fatal" accident had reached distant strangers, actually happened to Lynn at Easter-time. She answered her phone, at work, in her usual manner—"This is Lynn, how can I help you?" The caller replied, "Hello Lynn, I used to live in Woodsville, but I moved to Florida a couple of years ago. I want to put a memorial message in the paper, in remembrance of the son that I lost in a car accident shortly before I left." With tears in her eyes, and a palpitating heart, Lynn compassionately saw to it that she got exactly what she wanted. They were mutually sharing farewells, when the caller surprised her with—"By the way, how's your son doing? We've been praying for him." Lynn was left speechless, as precious tears of joy gently caressed her blushing cheeks. She politely ended the call, grabbed a tissue to wipe the tears, and blankly stared at the inscription on a wooden carving hanging on the wall beside her desk—"*AND NOW THESE THREE REMAIN: FAITH, HOPE AND LOVE. BUT THE GREATEST OF THESE IS LOVE.*"

CHAPTER 24:   A NEW BEGINNING

The end of Jimmy's first life began with his request to change his parents' vacation plans from the beach to New York City. After which, he insisted on having the three screws removed from his leg—because he could never have a full-body MRI. A couple of hours before the accident, he assured his mom that he would be home by his curfew—if he wasn't hit by a car.

He was not home by his curfew, because he was struck by an SUV. Several hours later, he had a full-body MRI. Jimmy's requested change in vacation plans took them to John Lennon's former place of residence in New York City. He returned to the world of the living listening to John Lennon's music.

The single set of footprints, Joe and Lynn had been seeing in their dreams, steadily reverted to the original set of two. Now, they found themselves standing, with wonderment and anticipation, on the threshold of a new beginning.

"Whisper words of wisdom, let it be.
There will be an answer."   . . .

CHAPTER 25: RESIDUAL TRANSITIONS

Rome wasn't built in a day, and everyone crawls before they walk. Jimmy's new lease on life will take time to develop and blossom. He went back to school, and successfully completed the first semester of his senior year. However, in actuality, he was completing the third trimester of his second gestation period. He was, at the time, facing the daunting challenges associated with the beginning of a new life, and it would not be an easy task. The time had come for him to crawl again.

His goal was to graduate from high school, but he did not want to go back. He firmly insisted on finding an alternative way to complete his quest. He told his mom, "I can't stand being in a place with a lot of people." She replied, "I will have to talk it over with your father." Lynn shared his feelings with Joe and they decided to contact the principal at the high school to inquire about the possibility of having him complete his graduation requirements at home. He only needed one credit in English, and one credit in math, to be eligible for a high school diploma. The principal was confident that something could be arranged, but she would need some paperwork completed by an accredited physician, who was treating him, before she could act on their request. Lynn hand-delivered the completed paperwork two days later, and the wheels were set in motion.

Exactly one week after receiving the required paperwork, a very qualified teacher was assigned to teach Jimmy at home. The teacher was all-business, and easy to get along with at the same time. Jimmy quickly adapted to his teacher's demeanor and style of teaching, and he passed. He legitimately earned his high school diploma—but, he refused to participate in the graduation exercises and commencement, because he only cared about obtaining his diploma and tassel. He wanted his diploma for obvious reasons, and he wanted the tassel to hang on the rearview mirror of the car he expected to be driving as soon as possible.

Approximately one month before Jimmy graduated from high school, Lynn contacted the professional driving instructor she had employed to get Jack ready for the road. She re-hired him, and he worked very hard to get Jimmy ready for the state mandated written and road tests. Jimmy passed his written test, his father assisted with the road-test-training process, and he passed the road test on his first attempt.

Jimmy was elated when he got his driver's license, after which he begged his parents to help him get a car. He told them that he needed a car to get a job, and they fell for it. They helped him purchase a dark blue Honda Civic with a lot of miles on it, but in decent condition, one week after he graduated from high school.

Fortunately, Jimmy found a job right away. His friend Dave, who was with him when he was struck by the SUV, was working at a Giant grocery store in Frederick, and he spoke to his boss about him. She simply said, "Tell your friend to apply, and I'll see what I could do." Jimmy applied for a job as a cashier, and two weeks later he was actively training for the position. Shortly thereafter, he became very frustrated because of an unyielding residual problem. He was having a hard time scanning and bagging the grocery items, because of the nerve damage in his right arm and hand.

In early October, Joe and Lynn went to New York to visit with Joe's father and go to Jack's homecoming football game. They left early on a Saturday morning; went to the game; spent an evening with Joe's father; and drove back home on Sunday. Joe was somewhat disappointed, because the home team lost and Jack didn't get a chance to play. Nevertheless, he was still on schedule to receive his Bachelor of Arts degree in the spring, and Joe wanted that for his son, and himself, more than football.

The trip home was pleasant, but Jimmy greeted his parents with some very upsetting news. He

said, "How was your trip? I quit my job at Giant."
Joe and Lynn felt like they knew it was going to
happen, because he started complaining about the
difficulties he was experiencing shortly after he
started working there, but they never expected it
to happen so soon.

Joe desperately wanted his son to enroll in
classes at the local community college, but he
sincerely believed that Jimmy lacked the
confidence, and self-esteem, that was necessary to
be successful. Joe and Lynn tried their best to
convince him that he was more than capable of
succeeding at the community college level, but he
just ignored them. He had a much larger residual
problem that he was planning on dealing with on
his own, and for the time being, the going to
school plan was indefinitely placed on hold.

Jimmy could not get over his fascination with
prescription medication. After he turned eighteen,
he relinquished his pediatrician for a general
practitioner—and, at his first appointment, he did
his best to convince his new doctor that he needed
narcotic-based medication for pain. The wise
physician, who treated his parents on a regular
basis, saw straight through his fake facade and
firmly denied his request.

Jimmy had a difficult time accepting the
failure of his planned ruse, and immediately
decided to take the matter into his own hands. He

convinced himself, with the assistance of research on the internet, that narcotic-based pain medication had too many side-effects, and marijuana was the way to go. His googled research also informed him that marijuana was legally being used to treat a variety of illnesses, and several states had legalized it for medicinal purposes. He was certain that he needed to stop taking most of his script-meds and replace them with weed. He immediately went in search of a local dealer who could supply him with marijuana, and it was relatively easy for him to find one who lived nearby.

His father had been giving him a twenty dollar allowance each week for many years, and he saved most of it in a lock-box that was hidden in his room. The very same box that housed the pipe he used to smoke weed in the not-so-distant past. He also had over a thousand dollars in a savings account, and more than three-hundred dollars in cash that he saved from the several paychecks he had earned at Giant. Therefore, in his mind, money was not going to be a problem. He coyly approached his mom and said, "I want to wean-off almost all of my meds." She was very pleased with his decision, and anxiously contacted the doctor who prescribed them. The doctor was very supportive and gave her detailed instructions related to the weaning process. It took two weeks for Jimmy to

wean himself off of the script-meds he had chosen
to replace with marijuana. In the between-time, he
started burning incense in his room to get his
parents accustomed to the odor that he intended to
use to mask the unmistakable smell of the weed he
planned on smoking.

A few months after he started treating his
symptoms with increasing amounts of marijuana, he
began to experience feelings of paranoia. To make
matters worse, he developed a very serious weight-
gaining problem due to the constant munchies he
was satisfying with the consumption of an
overabundance of snacks he had squirreled away in
his room. He added more than fifty pounds of
excess fat to his former slim and trim body in
less than nine months. On his nineteenth birthday,
he weighed almost sixty pounds more than his ideal
weight and he was quickly taking his feelings of
paranoia in the wayward direction of a nervous
breakdown.

Jimmy's partial nervous breakdown, in the
summer, nearly escalated to an unrelenting state
of psychosis when he suddenly realized that he
just needed to get out of Woodsville and the state
of Maryland. He strategically removed each of the
posters that his dad had put in his room,
initially at his request, and said, "It's time for
me to move on and get as far away from Woodsville
as possible. I need to get far away from

everything that happened to me." His dilemma
closely resembled a very common trait exhibited by
many individuals who have endured the
circumstances surrounding a similar traumatic
event. He boldly approached his mother and
demanded, "You need to ask your parents if I could
move in with them." Lynn made the phone call and
her mom instantly said, "Yes."

Jimmy quickly packed everything he thought he
would need; and, on a pleasant-weather weekend in
mid-August, his parents anxiously drove him to the
family farm in Buena Vista, Virginia. Jimmy's
maternal grandparents welcomed him with opened
arms. They were genuinely honored to have the
grandchild, who had survived what should have been
a fatal accident, spend some time with them. Joe
and Lynn left their youngest son with tears in
their eyes, because they were very worried about
where his chosen path might lead him. Joe
curiously pondered the possibility that everything
might somehow be related to something ethereal.

Jimmy excitedly settled in at what he truly
believed to be his new home. His grandparents knew
better, but they were just as happy to have him as
he was to be there. They did everything they could
to make him feel welcomed. His grandmother gave
him some chores to do around the house, and he
surprised her by doing an outstanding job. His

grandfather taught him how to make baskets, and
burn downed trees.

Jimmy sincerely enjoyed his tree-burning
experience, but he was longing for an even more
exciting adventure. He wanted to learn how to hunt
small game animals; so, he humbly approached his
grandfather and asked, "Will you take me squirrel
hunting?" Unfortunately, hunting was not an
integral part of his grandfather's vast repertoire
of talents. He possessed the knowledge and
experience, but he had never enjoyed it—and his
failing health precluded his participation in such
a strenuous activity. However, he was also very
stubborn, and come hell or high water, he was not
going to disappoint his grandson. The church he
attended was sponsoring a weeklong retreat for
young people, and he decided to offer his grandson
a compromise. He replied, "If you will go to the
retreat that my church is hosting for people your
age, then I will take you hunting when it's over."
Jimmy curiously questioned his grandfather, "What
should I expect?" He said, "You will get to mingle
with people your own age and gain some valuable
experience that you will never forget."

Jimmy decided to go to the retreat, and he
did not regret his decision. He thoroughly enjoyed
himself, and he gained some valuable experience.
Several retreaters attempted to entice him into
smoking weed, and he politely said, "Thanks, but

I'm not into that." He calmly reminisced about the circumstances that had initially forced him to leave home—when he was smoking weed and getting paranoid, and he wisely chose not to go down that path again. Fortunately, his decision ultimately helped him gain the respect of the teenagers who had unintentionally attempted to divert him.

After the retreat, he anxiously returned to his grandparents' home hoping for that opportunity to go hunting, and he was not disappointed. In the early morning, of the following day, his grandfather lived up to his end of the deal. They both put on their orange hunting vests and headed-out, with 22-caliber rifles, in search of squirrels. The squirrels were hiding, so grandpa calmly suggested that they take some target practice at a few tree limbs. Jimmy really did not care if he shot at a squirrel or a tree—he just wanted to shoot a gun. He got his wish; and, for the time being, his grandfather was his hero.

When Jimmy arrived at the family farm, in mid-August, he was almost sixty pounds overweight. He used the majority of his over-abundant amount of free time to exercise. He explored almost every inch of the hilly 300 acres that he could safely navigate; he made good use of his grandparents' exercise equipment; he consumed a healthy diet; and, by mid-November, he had lost all the weight he had gained. He once again pushed the scale to the same 158 pounds that he weighed more than three years ago, on that fateful evening, when he was struck by the SUV.

Jimmy's maternal grandparents had successfully helped him turn his life around. He was doing daily chores; he graciously offered his assistance at mealtime; he bowed his head when his grandfather said grace; and he went to church every Sunday. He had only experienced that type of lifestyle, with his undevout catholic parents, on Thanksgiving, Christmas, and Easter. More importantly, he had successfully weaned himself off of the weed that had made him paranoid enough to want to leave home in the first place.

Joe had initially reasoned that Jimmy would want to return home by Halloween. The Thanksgiving holiday was quickly approaching, and Lynn surprisingly received a phone call from her capricious son. He said, "I want to spend Thanksgiving here, and then I want to come home." Lynn was much more than elated. She excitedly shared the good news with Joe, who matter-of-factly responded, "Thanksgiving was my second guess. We'll have to drive down there on Black Friday and bring him home on Saturday."

CHAPTER 26:   THE NEXT TO LAST RESIDUAL

Joe and Lynn brought Jimmy home on the Saturday after Thanksgiving. He was not the same person who had insisted on leaving back in August. He almost annoyingly offered to help around the house in any way that he could. When Joe was making dinner, he offered to help set the table. When Lynn was cleaning the house, he consistently asked her, "How can I help?" They were not accustomed to his benevolent offers for assistance, but they politely accommodated his benign wishes on each and every occasion.

Unfortunately, Jimmy's desire to help had directly been influenced by Lynn's delegating parents and it would not last. In the second week of December, Jimmy's offers suddenly stopped, and he slipped into the throes of a deep depression. He would sleep past noon and refuse to shower, brush his teeth, or change his clothes. Lynn began to worry; so, she decided to contact Jimmy's doctor and solicit his advice. He told her that she should get in touch with a psychiatrist, and he recommended a Frederick practitioner who would accept her insurance. Lynn immediately contacted the psychiatrist's office and quickly secured an appointment.

The first appointment was, for the most part, an information seeking session. Jimmy kept complaining about having trouble sleeping, and he disappointedly left with a prescription for Ambien. The psychiatrist met with him once a week for the next few weeks. She thoroughly questioned him, attentively listened to his answers, and subjected him to a battery of common psychoanalytical tests.

In the middle of his fourth appointment, she abruptly stopped and said, "I need to ask your mom to join us." Jimmy replied, "OK." She politely thanked him, went to the waiting room to get his mother, and got down to business. She said, "Jimmy is battling with Post-Traumatic-Stress-Disorder, and I want to treat it with a combination of medication and therapy." Jimmy interrupted, "The Ambien isn't working." She retaliated with, "You're probably right, because your condition can only be treated with medication in conjunction with regular sessions with a qualified therapist." Jimmy said, "I won't take any medicine for depression." She asked, "Why not?" He replied, "Depression medications have too many bad side effects." She tried to explain the reasoning behind her decision, "PTSD manifests itself in ways that tend to vary widely with each patient. The best way to treat it depends on the individual patient's symptoms. All medicines have side effects, some worse than others, but you are suffering from a combination of PTSD fueled anxiety and depression and you need to be simultaneously treated for both." Jimmy replied, "OK, I'll try anything that you think might help me." The psychiatrist wrote the prescriptions and handed them to Lynn. Jimmy made an appointment with the therapist, and they got the prescriptions filled on their way home.

Jimmy cooperatively participated in his weekly sessions with his therapist, and he regularly consumed his prescribed doses of valium and clonazepam for anxiety—but, he refused to take the medicine for depression. Joe was concerned about the possibility that his son might become dependent on prescription drugs, because of the manipulative tactics he had obviously employed to obtain prescription narcotic painkillers in the past. He decided to question his son about the medicine he was taking. Jimmy replied, "Don't worry dad, I'm trying my best to talk my doctor into taking me off all my meds, because I hate the side-effects. That's why I won't take the depression medicine she prescribed." Joe curiously asked, "What side-effects?" Jimmy said, "Nausea, constipation, weight-gain, thoughts of suicide, and liver damage—just to name a few—even death." Joe asked, "How did you learn about the side-effects?" Jimmy said, "I like to research medicine on the internet." Joe immediately recognized an opportunity to make a valuable suggestion, "Jimmy,

I have to commend you on your knowledge of medicine and their side-effects. I sincerely believe that you could easily find a way to turn your interest in prescription medication into a career." Jimmy wanted to know more, and asked, "What do you mean?" Joe answered, "You could take one class at the community college that will prepare you for the Pharmacy Technician Certification Exam." Jimmy said, "Tell me more." Joe replied, "If you take the class and pass the exam, then you will be state certified as a legal drug dealer." Jimmy became very interested. Joe went on to elaborate, "You would be fully qualified for a job in any pharmacy, hospital or nursing home in the state." Jimmy asked, "What about out-of-state jobs?" Joe paused for a moment and said, "I am not aware of any out-of-state restrictions, but I would have to look into it." Jimmy asked, "When would I take the class?" Joe logged onto the Frederick Community College website, quickly found the answer, and said, "Sixteen sessions are scheduled to begin on the 17th of June and end on the 23rd of August." Jimmy replied, "I want to do it, but I need to run it by my therapist before I make a decision." Joe was impressed by his son's logic and quickly responded, "You have my full support."

In the midst of some unusually wicked weather that pounded the Frederick area in February, Jimmy secured his therapist's blessings to pursue a career as a pharmacy technician. In that same time period, he coerced his psychiatrist into letting him take his medication on an "as-needed" basis. The fifty-plus inches of wind-driven snow, must have somehow cleared the air—because Jimmy appeared to be poised to put the memory of his traumatic experience in the past, and look ahead to a potentially promising future.

The welcomed April showers casually carried Jimmy over the threshold of indifference—by somehow converting his past interests into a committed desire to make his life count for something. Early in the month of April, when Joe was on spring break, Jimmy politely asked, "Will you please take me to the community college to register for the pharmacy technician class?" Joe was beside himself when he excitedly said, "Yes." In the early afternoon, on a Wednesday, Joe happily helped his son register for the class and pay the tuition.

Jimmy drove himself to each class, participated in the class discussions, asked relevant questions, and seriously developed a strong interest in the potential career he was actively pursuing. During that time, Joe was working on a home-improvement project, but he always dropped what he was doing whenever his

son needed help with his homework. Jimmy completed
the course, near the top of his class, and he
could hardly wait to take the certification exam.
He took the exam on a Monday, in early October,
and he passed. Less than a month later, he secured
part-time employment, as a pharmacy technician, at
the very same Rite Aid pharmacy that had been
filling his prescriptions.

Throughout his first year, Jimmy did a
stellar job as a part-time pharmacy technician. In
early November, the pharmacist told him that he
should go back to school to become a full-fledged
pharmacist, and Jimmy took the complimentary
suggestion very seriously. However, shortly
thereafter, his mother came home from work with
advance knowledge of an ad that was going in the
newspaper for a full-time pharmacy technician at
the Woodsville Nursing Home. Upon hearing the
news, Jimmy said, "Thank you, I am very
interested." She suggested, "You should wait until
the ad is published and then apply for the job. It
is scheduled to run in the paper this Thursday."
Jimmy said, "OK, I will."

The Woodsville Nursing Home, on Route 176,
was located a little less than one mile South of
Jimmy's violent collision with the SUV. He applied
for the position, and he received a phone call,
less than 24 hours later, to schedule an
interview.

Jimmy was a little nervous about how he would be perceived at his interview. He wore the same suit he had donned for his sister's wedding, and he decided to drive himself. Marlania, the young lady who interviewed him, assured him, "I will get in touch with you before the end of the week." As he was driving home, he thought about his pretty interviewer, a curvaceous blonde with hazel eyes, and the answers he gave to her questions. By the time he arrived home, he was feeling very good about himself because she was not wearing a wedding ring, and he was confident that he responded to her questions in an honest and professional manner. His feelings were justified, on the following day, when he unexpectedly received a phone call from Marlania. She said, "I want to hire you. Can you start this coming Monday?" He was almost speechless, and he was shaking with excitement when he said, "Yes, thank you." Somehow sensing how he was feeling, she said, "Relax, you've got the job and I need you to come in no later than Friday to complete the paperwork." He excitedly replied, "I will see you tomorrow."

Less than a week after he started working there, he questioned his father about the elderly patients who did not appear to recognize the family members that came to visit them. Joe answered, "They are probably suffering from

Alzheimer's." Jimmy conscientiously said, "Dad, I really wish that there was something I could do to help them." Joe said, "Trust me son, my grandmother had Alzheimer's and she thought I was her husband, who was my grandfather, when I went to visit her at a nursing home. What you are witnessing is very real. Alzheimer's is a terrible disease."

CHAPTER 27: A PLAUSIBLE REASON

Jimmy's alarm woke him, on Monday morning, to remind him that it was time to get ready for work. He had no memory of the mysterious writing that transpired during the night. He took a short shower, combed his hair, brushed his teeth, and went back to his room to get dressed. While he was getting dressed, he noticed the out of place notebook on top of his desk. With a very curious look on his face, he slowly reached for the notebook. He picked it up; recognized his own handwriting; read what he had apparently written; and immediately placed it, along with the feather, in the top left drawer of his desk. Then, he calmly finished dressing and followed his morning ritual. He made a pot of coffee and consumed a bowl of organic cereal with fat-free milk. After his second cup of coffee, he said goodbye to Zoso and left for work.

When he returned home, Joe was in the kitchen doing prep-work for dinner. Jimmy walked into the kitchen and said, "Dad, I need you to look at something." His father asked, "Can it wait?" Jimmy said, "No." Joe said, "OK Jimmy, let me see what you've got." He went upstairs to his room and pulled the sheet of paper, with the mysterious writing on it, out of the notebook. Then, he went back downstairs to the kitchen and handed it to his father.

Cure AD

40% $(CH_6)_4O_2S$

30% Cod Liver Oil

15% Oleic Acid

12% Prune Juice

3% Lecithin

Joe quickly read it and curiously asked, "Where did you get this?" Jimmy answered, "It's my handwriting—I found it on top of my desk this morning, and I don't know how it got there." Joe said, "Thank you for sharing this with me. I will need some time to think about it." Jimmy replied, "Take all the time you need."

Later, that same evening, Joe showed the mysterious writing to Lynn and queried, "What do you make of this? Jimmy found it on his desk when he got up this morning, and he does not recall writing it." Lynn said, "I really don't know. You should google the ingredients."

Joe googled $(CH_6)_4O_2S$ and discovered that the chemical, to the best of google's knowledge, did not exist. After which, he separately googled each of the listed ingredients with some enlightening results. "Cod liver oil contains the elongated omega-3 fatty acid DHA which is extremely important in the development and function of the brain and nervous system, and has been proven to be a powerhouse in fighting disease. Oleic acid, a chemical constituent of olive oil, improves the integrity of cell membranes by allowing them to maintain a liquid-crystalline state, even in adverse conditions, which promotes cell membrane fluidity. Prune juice is high in antioxidants, called phenols, which aid in blocking oxygen-based free radicals from damaging the body's crucial fats. It is also an excellent source of potassium. Lecithin, a phospholipid, chemically known as phosphatidylcholine, is a principal component of nearly all cell membranes."

Joe carefully reviewed his research and reasoned that the AD in Jimmy's handwritten message might stand for Alzheimer's Disease—after which, he sensibly decided to google Alzheimer's to see if he could ascertain a connection. He learned that the latest research on Alzheimer's was focusing on a normally soluble string of amino acids called B-amyloid that is illogically being transformed into an insoluble form, which effectively blocks the movement of potassium through the cell membranes of afflicted individuals—a condition referred to as potassium

channel dysfunction. Further research confirmed
the insoluble B-amyloid/potassium channel
dysfunction theory. Two enzymes, beta secretase
and gamma secretase, clip insoluble B-amyloid
strings of amino acids out of a larger, and
entirely normal, parent molecule—amyloid precursor
protein. The strings of insoluble B-amyloid clump
to form the plaques that cause potassium channel
dysfunction. Brain cells that cannot get the
potassium they need to function properly lose
their ability to effectively communicate with each
other, and the electrochemical impulses which are
normally transmitted through the spaces between
the cells come to halt. The end result is
Alzheimer's Disease.

Joe was convinced that the AD in Jimmy's
mysterious writing stood for Alzheimer's Disease,
and that it might contain the formula for a
chemical cocktail that could somehow be used to
treat it. He shared his belief with Lynn, and
requested her opinion. Lynn replied, "Right now, I
don't have an opinion. I want to know why Jimmy
wrote it, and where it came from." Joe obviously
could not give her an answer. He said, "Lynn, I'm
curious about the chemical that apparently doesn't
exist. I firmly believe that Jimmy is telling the
truth, and we should attempt to locate someone who
could help us find the answers to our questions."
Lynn quickly said, "I have an idea. I know a lady,

who works at Fort Detrick, who might be able to help us. Do you remember Jenny talking about Kathy when she was going to school and working there?" Joe answered, "No." Lynn replied, "Well, Jenny worked with Kathy at Fort Detrick back then, and they still keep in touch with one another. As a matter of fact, Jenny recently told me that Kathy still works there, and she had lunch with her a couple of weeks ago. I'll give Kathy a call and see if there is anything she could do to help us."

On Wednesday, November 27, Lynn phoned Kathy at Fort Detrick and briefly described the dilemma. Kathy told Lynn to email the chemical formula to her, and she would forward it to each of their biochemists—along with a request for any information they could send her. Then, she assured Lynn that she would forward any replies. They exchanged email addresses—Lynn humbly expressed her gratitude and appreciation, and pressed the end button on her cell phone.

One week later, as promised, Lynn received a few replies via forwarded email. Two biochemists simply categorized the empirical formula as a fictional compound. However, one biochemist, Dr. Gustov Putin wrote, "To the best of my knowledge, the compound does not exist. Contact Dr. Nikolai Rostov at the National Center for Stem Cell Research (NCSCR), located in Woodsville, and request his opinion." Lynn shared the news with

Joe, who immediately volunteered to try to get an appointment with Dr. Rostov. Joe was very familiar with the location of the NCSCR building on East Baltimore Street, which runs parallel to the route 176 Woodsville bypass. He said, "The NCSCR building is close to where Jimmy had his face to face with the SUV, and less than a half-mile North of the nursing home where he works."

On Monday, December 8, Joe stopped at the NCSCR on his way home from work, and went in to see if he could get an appointment with Dr. Rostov. A female receptionist, sitting at a desk located just inside the entrance, greeted him with a Russian accent, "How can I help you?" Joe smiled and said, "I hope you can. My name is Joe Masden and I would like to make an appointment to speak with Dr. Rostov." She asked, "Why would you like to meet with him?" He quickly replied, "My wife and I contacted Dr. Putin, at Fort Detrick, for some information regarding a formula for a chemical compound that no one seems to think exists, and he highly recommended that we contact Dr. Rostov." The receptionist took her phone off the hook and pressed a button to make a call. Someone answered, and she said, "It's Natasha, I have a man here who wants to make an appointment to speak with you about some unknown chemical compound. He is claiming that Dr. Putin recommended you." Immediately thereafter, she hung the phone up, looked Joe straight in the eye, and said, "Please follow me, Dr. Rostov will see you now." Preparedly armed with Jimmy's handwritten formula in his coat pocket, Joe followed the black-haired, shapely, beauty down the empty hallway that led to Dr. Rostov's office. Natasha knocked twice on the door, opened it, and said, "Dr. Rostov, this is Mr. Masden." Dr. Rostov's heavy Russian accent did not surprise Joe when he heard him say, "Please come in and have a seat. How can I help you?" Joe entered and began to sit in the lone seat situated in the front of Dr. Rostov's desk. He suddenly stopped, extended his right hand, and said, "Joe Masden." Dr. Rostov slowly lifted his barrel-shaped body out of his seat, extended his right hand and replied, "Nikolai Rostov, It is my pleasure to meet you." They shook hands and sat down. Joe could not help but notice Dr. Rostov's bushy eyebrows and round facial features that reminded him of his own Austro-Hungarian grandparents.

Joe said, "A little over six years ago, my son was violently struck by an SUV on Route 176, a short distance North of here, and he miraculously survived. He sustained a minor brain injury, but not a single bone was broken. Later on, he successfully endured a couple of years of therapy, specifically designed to help him overcome the post traumatic stress that nearly broke him. A little over two years ago, he became certified as a pharmacy technician, and he is presently employed at the Woodsville Nursing Home just South of here. A couple of weeks ago, he handed me a piece of paper on which he claimed to have unknowingly written some mysterious medicinal instructions that I believe may be useful in treating Alzheimer's Disease. My belief is based on the fact that the empirical formula for one of the chemicals in the "cocktail" is apparently nonexistent. Dr. Putin, at Fort Detrick, confirmed the nonexistence of the chemical in an email in which he recommended that you should be contacted."

Joe took Jimmy's handwritten formula out of his coat pocket, and anxiously handed it to Dr. Rostov. Dr. Rostov carefully read the apparent recipe for the ingredients that could "Cure AD" and took a brief moment to contemplate his reply. Then, he asked, "Does your son have any background in chemistry?" Joe answered, "He has never even taken a class in chemistry." Dr. Rostov raised his dark, bushy eyebrows and said, "It is possible that you might be on to something. To the best of my knowledge, $(CH_6)_4O_2S$ does not exist. I am going to refer you to a comrade of mine, Dr. Yuri Matzin, who is part of a Russian-Canadian-American team of scientists who are actively pursuing a cure for Alzheimer's. Dr. Matzin is doing his research at the Brain Research Centre in Vancouver, British Columbia, and he is a world-renowned expert in the synthesis of chemical compounds. I am going to give you his email address, and I will email him with a "heads-up" synopsis. When you email him, please mention that it was I who recommended that you contact him." Then, he handed Joe a piece of paper and said, "Please be sure to include a copy of your son's mysterious formula as an attachment." They both stood up and shook hands. Joe thanked him for his help, assured him that he would follow his advice, and quickly left to go home.

A couple of days later, on Wednesday, December 11, Joe sent Dr. Matzin the following email:

Dr. Matzin: My name is Joe Masden and I recently met with Dr. Nikolai Rostov at the National Center for Stem Cell Research, who recommended that I contact you. I have mysteriously stumbled upon a mixture of chemicals that may, in some way, effectively treat Alzheimer's Disease. My hypothesis, as ridiculous as it may seem, revolves around the presence of an unknown chemical in the overall formula that may play a critical role. Dr. Putin, at Fort Detrick, and Dr. Rostov have both confirmed the chemical's nonexistence. My youngest son "unknowingly" wrote the attached handwritten "cocktail" with the heading "Cure AD." It is my sincere wish that you could, at your convenience, somehow synthesize the unknown chemical and test the formula. I am looking forward to hearing from you, as I greatly value your opinion. Sincerely, Joe Masden

Joe did not have to wait very long. Exactly one week later, on Wednesday, December 18, he received the following email from Dr. Matzin:

Mr. Masden: I want to thank you for contacting me and sending me your son's formula. I have successfully synthesized the unknown chemical, which I have named 4-hexamethyl dioxysulfide (MHOS) and I am currently calibrating the formula to test on lab rats with varying degrees of Alzheimer's. I will email you with the preliminary results. Dr. Matzin

Joe, again, did not have to wait too long. Less than one week later, on Christmas Eve, Dr. Matzin emailed him with some very exciting news.

Mr. Masden: All of the tested lab rats, with varying degrees of Alzheimer's, appear to be completely normal. I have tested blood and urine samples taken from the experimental groups with some astounding results. Each of the samples tested positive for a soluble form of B-amyloid, which was not found in any samples obtained from the control groups. As promising as it might seem, I cannot be certain that your son's formula is responsible for the apparent results until I perform comparative autopsies of the rat's brains. After I complete the autopsies, I will email you with my conclusion. Dr. Matzin

On Friday, January 3, Joe received the following email from Dr. Matzin.

Mr. Masden: I have completed the autopsies, and I am confident that MHOS chemically changed the insoluble form of B-amyloid into a soluble form that could diffuse into the circulatory system and be removed by the kidneys. The experimental rats' brains were completely free of insoluble B-amyloid plaques and clumps called oligomers. The control rats' brains were littered with the insoluble plaques and clumps. I believe that the rest of your son's formula probably assists in rejuvenating the permeability of aged nerve cell membranes, because they are irreplaceable. The next step is to retest the formula on a new group of Alzheimer afflicted rats, and observe them as they live out their lives, in an effort to ascertain the probability of any long-term side effects. In the meantime, I would like to make arrangements to meet with you and your son. The Brain Research Centre is more than willing to pay for your travel, meals, and accommodations. Please email me ASAP with a tentative time-frame for your visit. Dr. Matzin

It was the wrong time of year for Joe, being a teacher, to plan on taking some time off from work—as the winter break had just ended. Joe and Lynn had weekends free, but Jimmy's work schedule varied and oftentimes had him working over the weekend. Joe did not know what to do or say, so he casually asked Jimmy if he could get some time off on a weekend to go to Canada and meet the doctor who was testing his formula. Jimmy told his dad that he would speak with his boss.

Jimmy spoke with the woman of his dreams on Monday, and she told him that he could have any weekend off that he wanted—all she needed was a couple of days notice. Jimmy gave his dad the good news when he returned home from work. Later that same evening, Joe shared the news with Lynn, and together they decided on the last weekend in January—weather permitting.

Joe emailed Dr. Matzin with the tentative date, mentioned that he would like his wife to accompany him, and emphasized the fact that it depended on the weather. Dr. Matzin replied:

Mr. Masden: I will make arrangements for a limousine to transport the three of you to Dulles Airport on Saturday, January 25. You will travel first class on an 8:00 AM EDT flight to Vancouver. You should arrive at Vancouver International around 10:00 AM PDT, where you will be met by an associate of mine who will transport the three of you to the Shangri-La Hotel in downtown Vancouver. I will meet with you in the hotel's restaurant, at 12:30 PM, for lunch. I am sincerely looking forward to meeting with you, your wife, and Jimmy. You will fly out of Vancouver International, Sunday morning at 6:00 AM PDT and arrive at Dulles around 2:00 PM EDT, where you will again be transported, by limousine, back to your home—all at no cost to you. Dr. Matzin

Joe emailed Dr. Matzin with his thanks, informed him that he was excited about getting the opportunity to meet him, and reminded him about the stipulation related to the weather.

CHAPTER 28: HIDEOUSLY HEINOUS

Dr. Rostov and Natasha had been having an affair for the past three years. It was initiated by Natasha, who was trying to destroy his marriage, so she could have him for herself. She slyly left plenty of tell-tale clues specifically designed to inform his wife of her husband's indiscretion. Dr. Rostov's wife easily recognized the meaning of the clues—but, rather than questioning him or hiring a private detective, she simply decided to get even by having an affair of her own. Natasha was dumbfounded, because she was completely unaware of the means by which Mrs. Rostov chose to cope with the situation.

Mrs. Rostov was out of the country, visiting with relatives in Moscow. Dr. Rostov and Natasha had just finished making love. Natasha was smoking a Russian cigarette, while Dr. Rostov was telling her about the success Dr. Matzin was having with the unknown chemical that Mr. Masden had shared with him. He said, "Dr. Matzin is ready to announce his preliminary findings to the world, but he wants to meet with the Masdens and get their son's permission to be included as a co-discoverer before he makes the announcement." The exciting news greatly upset Natasha, who openly hated all Americans and what she deemed to be their highfalutin, better than thou, attitude. She used her nearly finished cigarette to light a new one and said, "Let me see if I have this right. You're telling me that Dr. Matzin synthesized the chemical, calibrated the formula, successfully used it to cure Alzheimer's in lab rats, and is ready to announce his findings to the world." Dr. Rostov replied, "In a nutshell—Yes." Natasha quickly asked, "Please explain to me why he would want to include this young man, who supposedly "dreamed-up" the formula, as a co-discoverer?" Dr. Rostov said, "Because Dr. Matzin is a good man, who is only trying to do what he believes is right. It is not up to us to question his obvious good intentions, but to accept them. Now, if you are finished with your senseless bickering, I would like to take a short nap." Natasha sweetly said, "Of course, darling." Then, she kissed him on his forehead, put her cigarette out in the ashtray on the nightstand, and gently positioned herself beside him.

Shortly afterwards, Dr. Rostov began snoring and Natasha bolted into action. She got out of bed and was putting her robe on as she quickly headed in the direction of Dr. Rostov's laptop. She sat in the chair at his desk and accessed his email account. Then, she clicked on the latest email from Dr. Matzin, and it contained the detailed information she was hoping to find in regards to the date, time, and place of the meeting he

planned on having with the Masdens. She opened a
desk drawer, removed a sticky note pad and pen,
and wrote the vital information down on the top
sheet. She pulled the sheet from the pad, placed
the pad and pen back in the drawer, and closed it.
Then, she rushed back into the bedroom, got
dressed, quickly kissed her sleeping lover on his
cheek, and quietly left.

After she arrived at her apartment, she sat
down on the couch in her living room and
immediately texted a message to her much older
brother—who was living with their father in
Moscow. "Go to a place where we can speak in
private and call me." Then, she drew herself a
bath and went into her bedroom, where she quickly
replaced her clothes with a blue silk bathrobe.
She brought her cell phone into the bathroom, and
placed it on the vanity next to the tub. As she
was cleansing herself of the day's activities, she
occasionally glanced at her cell phone.
Unfortunately, it did not play the Russian
National Anthem she was anxiously waiting to hear.
After she finished bathing, she followed her
nightly beauty ritual and returned to the living
room. She placed her cell phone on the coffee
table, and went into the kitchen to make herself a
vodka on the rocks. She brought her drink into the
living room, took a sip, placed it on a coaster on
the coffee table and took a seat on the couch.

Then, she took her TV remote off of the coffee table and pressed the on button. She accessed the TV Guide channel and was viewing her options, when her cell phone started playing her favorite tune. She grabbed it and anxiously viewed the screen that displayed, "Call From Dimitri". She answered the call whispering, "Are you alone?" Dimitri said, "Yes, What's going on?" She replied, "We are in the midst of a critical international situation that only you, my dear brother, could bring to a satisfactory resolution." He asked, "What do you mean?" She said, "A little over a month ago, an American man came into the NCSCR and questioned Dr. Rostov about an unknown chemical that his son had "dreamed-up." Dr. Rostov suggested that he email Dr. Matzin in Vancouver, Canada, and the man followed his advice. Dr. Matzin subsequently synthesized the chemical and successfully used it to cure Alzheimer's in lab rats. He believes that it will work on humans, and he is ready to announce his findings. The crisis lies in the fact that he is more than willing to share his success with the American who "dreamed-up" the formula, and did nothing more. He has made arrangements to meet with the young man and his parents, in Vancouver, in just a few weeks from now. I have fortunately managed to obtain some detailed information regarding the arrangements and itinerary." Dimitri asked, "What does any of this have to do with me?" Natasha said, "My dear brother, I know that you despise the selfish, greedy, Americans—at least as much as I do—and I am confident that you would not want them getting any credit for a discovery as big as this; especially when a Russian did all the work. I want you to eliminate the three of them, and somehow convince Dr. Matzin into taking all the credit for himself." Dimitri smiled, and his spine tingled with excitement. It had been quite a long time since he last had the opportunity to be the top-notch assassin he was trained to be. He said, "I am having a hard time believing that your plan will be successful—but, I read you loud and clear. Please, give me all the details." Natasha gave him the date, time, and place for the meeting, and said, "You must not tell anyone—not even our father. I am certain that he would not approve." Dimitri replied, "I agree. The "old man" would never approve of eliminating anyone who was not a genuine threat to our family's well-being or the security of our country. I can assure you that I will not say anything to anyone." Natasha said, "I know I can trust you. Please, contact me after you have completed your mission, and have safely returned home." Dimitri replied, "Thank you—I will," and pressed the end button on his cell phone.

Dimitri and his father, Ivan, both served
their defunct country as outstanding KGB agents—
but, they lost their jobs when the Soviet Union
collapsed and the KGB was dissolved. Ivan was a
true statesman, who firmly honored his belief that
it was his duty to do whatever was necessary in
defense of his country. Dimitri, on the other
hand, was a sort of renegade—who took pride in the
fact that he was the only KGB agent who "always
got his man." He had, one way or another,
successfully managed to assassinate every target
he was assigned to eliminate. His last assignment
was around twenty-four years ago, and he was very
excited to have the unexpected opportunity to
resume his role as the undefeated assassin.

Dimitri was alone in his bedroom, and he went
straight to work planning the untimely deaths of
three innocent Americans. He conveniently had, in
his possession, the advanced prototype of an
umbrella-weapon that a Bulgarian inventor had
given him shortly after the collapse of the Soviet
Union. It was capable of firing a miniscule, but
fatal, splinter-shaped pellet—0.87 mm long and
0.68 mm wide at its widest point—containing 0.2 mg
of ricin into an unsuspecting victim. The pellet
was tightly wrapped in a heat-activated soluble
paper that was coated with a fast-acting
anesthetic. The weapon had been skillfully
designed to carry up to six shots of the

undetectable lethal poison. An insulated spring-
loaded mechanism silently changed chambers, and a
CO_2 cartridge produced more than enough silent
force to painlessly inject a clueless victim, in
close proximity, without touching them. Of utmost
importance was the fact that the Masdens would not
develop any symptoms until after they returned
home. Shortly thereafter, they would surely
perish. There would be a tiny red spot at the
injection site, which would quickly be noticed by
a coroner performing an autopsy—especially when
three closely related victims apparently died
from the same cause. However, unlike the previous
pellets made of a platinum-iridium alloy, the
heat-activated soluble splinters would completely
dissipate and leave the cause of death up to
speculation. The coroner could never prove that
they were poisoned with ricin. Dimitri firmly
believed that Jimmy would ultimately get the
credit he duly deserved. He just did not know how
to tell his naive sister, and he didn't care. He
was very anxiously anticipating something he has
longed for—the thrill of the kill.

At the appointed time, Dimitri told his
father that he was going to America to visit
Natasha. He departed from Moscow's Sheremetyevo
International Airport and landed at Baltimore's
BWI Airport. Shortly thereafter, he boarded a
plane to Canada's Vancouver International Airport.

He landed in Vancouver on Friday, January 24th—one day before the Masdens—because he wanted to scope out the hotel and plan his strategy. He checked-in with the concierge, declined assistance, carried his garment bag over his left shoulder, and pulled his rolling suitcase to the elevator. He took the elevator up to the 10th floor, located room 1004, and used his key-card to enter. He hung the garment bag that held a suit, dress shirt, tie, and black leather belt in the closet. He placed his suitcase on the king-sized bed, opened it, and slowly removed its contents. He hung the umbrella-weapon in the closet, and placed his dress shoes and an extra pair of sneakers on the closet's floor. He put two pairs of jeans, two casual tee-shirts, two undershirts, two boxers, and two pairs of socks in different dresser drawers. Then, he took a small black leather travel bag—that housed his shaving gear, toothbrush, medicine, vitamins, deodorant, and cologne—into the bathroom, and placed it on the vanity. He took a quick shower, casually dressed in a pair of jeans, a green tee-shirt, and sneakers, and left his room to physically examine the hotel's layout.

His thorough examination of the hotel's lobby; stairwells; elevators; water fountains; exercise room; pool area; and multiple restaurants with restrooms; pleased him. He reasoned that the elevator areas, and restaurants, would

logistically afford him with the highest
percentage of opportunities that he needed to
complete his mission. After which, he returned to
his room to get his coat, so he could go outside
and study the area near the hotel's entrance. He
visualized the drop-off area, and the walk through
the hotel's front doors to the concierge desk, as
two more reasonable opportunities. Then, he went
back to his room to phone an escort service and
plan an evening of fun.

The Masdens landed in Vancouver, in the mid-
morning of the following day, on schedule. Dr.
Matzin's associate promptly greeted them, and
assisted in loading their luggage into the trunk
of a rented black Cadillac CTS sedan. Then, they
quickly sped-off in the direction of the Shangri-
La Hotel.

It was drizzling a misty rain that was
forecasted to continue into the night. Dimitri was
anxiously waiting for them to arrive, near the
hotel's entrance, with his—due to the inclement
weather—rather inconspicuous umbrella-weapon in
hand. The Cadillac, transporting the unsuspecting
Masdens, pulled into the canopy-covered drop-off
area. Dimitri experienced a sharp, cramp-like pain
in his lower abdomen and a gurgling sensation in
his stomach. He had to quickly locate a restroom,
so he rushed into the hotel's lobby and jogged to
the closest restroom. He went into an open stall,

pulled his pants down, sat on the toilet, and let
it go. The obnoxious sounds were embarrassing, and
the putrid smell was disgusting, but the relief
was welcome. He flushed the toilet in a vain
attempt to rid the stall of its stench. Beads of
sweat dripped from his forehead, and he had no
choice but to sit there and try to regain his
composure.

In the meantime, the pre-registered Masdens
bypassed the concierge and were quickly ushered,
along with their luggage, into an open elevator.
Dr. Matzin's efficient associate pressed the
button for the 15th floor. The elevator doors
closed, and Joe noticed that there was no button
for a 13th floor. Joe said, "I don't see a button
for the 13th floor. Is that because of superstition
or tradition?" Dr. Matzin's associate said, "I am
not sure, but I would assume that it was some form
of tradition. You are staying in the Presidential
Suite, with exceptional amenities and two separate
bedrooms. We have done everything possible to make
your privacy a priority. The Brain Research
Centre's director has a security team stationed in
the hotel, and the concierge desk will not
transfer any phone calls or give your room number
to anyone."

Dimitri was still trying to recover on the
toilet in the lobby's restroom, when he felt
another gurgling sensation on the left-side of his

abdomen. A second round of obnoxious sounds and disgusting odor quickly followed. After which, the sweating subsided and he felt relieved. He sat there for a few moments, to be sure, and then proceeded to clean himself. He flushed the toilet, pulled his pants up, left the stall, and approached a sink to wash his hands. He was washing his hands while the Masdens were unpacking their luggage. He had lost his first opportunity to succeed in his quest. He quickly walked out of the restroom and rushed to the elevators. He was hoping to get a glimmer of a glimpse that might, in the very least, reveal the floor where the Masdens were staying. The lights for both elevators unfortunately indicated that they were patiently waiting for passengers in the lobby.

He immediately approached Peter, the young man in charge of the concierge desk, and very politely asked, "Excuse me—would you please give me the room number where my good friends, the Masdens, are staying?" Peter recognized Dimitri as a hotel guest, pretended to check a guest list, and intentionally lied, "No one going by that name is staying here. Are you certain that you have the right hotel?" Dimitri glared at Peter, and, with a touch of sarcasm, replied, "Perhaps not." Then, he casually returned to his room to lie down and wait for the scheduled 12:30 PM lunch meeting.

Peter immediately phoned Julio, the leader of the Masdens' security team, and informed him of the presence of a hotel guest who had questioned him regarding the Masdens' whereabouts. Julio rushed to meet with Peter—to get some more detailed information. Peter said, "The man's name is Dimitri Karloff, and he is staying in room 1004. He speaks with a heavy Russian accent, and he's about 5'10" with mostly gray hair, bushy eyebrows, and a stocky build. He checked-in yesterday and he is scheduled to check-out tomorrow." Julio politely asked, "Would you please do me a favor?" Peter answered, "Certainly, anything I can do to help." Julio said, "Thank you, I need you to call Dimitri's room. If he answers, tell him that you must have gotten the wrong number and hang-up." Peter phoned Dimitri, but he did not answer. Julio asked him to try again, and, after several rings, Dimitri answered. Peter asked, "Is this room 1005?" Dimitri said "No," and hung-up. Peter pressed the end button on the phone and said, "He's there." Julio responded, "Thank you very much. I will be sure to leave a good word about you with your boss." He immediately contacted his team, and they went to the 10th floor to keep an eye on room 1004 and develop a plan. Without hesitation, they mutually decided to station one man on the 10th floor, and a second man near the lobby elevators. Julio

stationed himself, on the 15th floor, just outside
of the Presidential Suite.

The Masdens took turns taking showers and
getting dressed. Jimmy went first, and his father
helped him with his tie while Lynn was taking her
shower. They were all dressed and ready to go at
noon. Jimmy wore the same brown suit he had donned
for his sister's wedding and job interview. Lynn
looked hot, for her age, dressed in a short-
skirted, deep purple, business suit that she had
purchased at Talbots of Frederick the day before
they left. Joe wore the same black suit he always
wore for any special occasion. In the past,
whenever Lynn had questioned him about his easily
predictable choice of attire, he always responded,
"I want you to bury me in this suit." A very
experienced assassin, who had changed into his
navy blue business suit, was patiently waiting in
the wings and skillfully planning on turning Joe's
sarcastic comment into a reality.

At 12:15 PM, the Masdens left their suite to
take the elevator down to the lobby and wait for
Dr. Matzin. Julio greeted them in the hallway. He
introduced himself as the leader of their security
team and told them that it was his duty to
accompany them to the lobby. Joe shook Julio's
hand and said, "Thank you." They walked to the
elevator and Julio pressed the down button. The
elevator doors opened—they went in—and Julio

pressed the button for the lobby. The elevator
doors closed and they began their descent. The
elevator suddenly stopped at the 10th floor and the
doors opened. Dimitri and the security guard were
standing there wanting to gain entrance. Julio
said, "You will have to wait for the next
elevator," and pressed the lobby button. Dimitri
made eye contact with Joe, and Joe sensed a
feeling of urgency in the strange man's eyes; the
doors closed and the elevator smoothly resumed its
descent to the lobby. The elevator arrived at its
destination, the doors opened, and the Masdens
casually walked into the lobby to wait for Dr.
Matzin.

They all took seats in the lobby. Lynn asked
Julio for any suggestions he might have for things
to do while they were there. Dimitri and the
security guard walked out of the elevator. Julio
said, "Please, give me a moment to think about
it," as he discreetly observed Dimitri. The
security guard went straight to the concierge desk
and made some small talk with Peter. Dimitri
casually glanced in the direction of the Masdens
and slowly made his way into the Lobby Lounge—
where the Matzin-Masden luncheon was scheduled to
be held. The security guard left his temporary
post, at the concierge desk, and rushed to the
lounge to keep an eye on him. Julio turned to Lynn
and said, "You will have to excuse me, as I am at

a loss for any ideas or suggestions. However, because you are scheduled to leave tomorrow morning, it is my recommendation that you take advantage of what the hotel has to offer. They have an indoor swimming pool, jacuzzis, hot tubs, saunas, and miniature golf. You also have fully-paid, gratuity-free, dinner reservations at Market by Jean-Georges—the hotel's premiere restaurant." Lynn thanked him and replied, "You seem to make perfect sense. Should I assume that it would also make your job easier? I don't mean to be sarcastic, or anything, but we could do each of those things at almost any hotel back in Maryland. This is the first out-of-country trip that we have been on in our lives, and we were really hoping to see more than the inside of a hotel."

At that moment, Dr. Matzin, and two other people, walked into the lobby. Julio excused himself and left to greet them. The Masdens left their seats and followed him. They all met in the center of the lobby—where they took turns introducing themselves and shaking hands. The Brain Research Centre's Public Relations Director, Michelle Felize, and Patent Attorney, Pierre LaChapelle, had accompanied him to take care of the business end of the meeting. Dr. Matzin led them to the entrance of the Lobby Lounge where the congenial hostess inquired, "Do you have a reservation?" Dr. Matzin replied, "Yes, it is in the name Matzin." The hostess checked her list, quickly procured six menus, and responded, "Please, follow me." The Matzin, party of six, obligingly followed her to their table.

Shortly after they were seated, a silent waiter filled their glasses with water and left. Shortly after that, a second waiter, Jacques, introduced himself and took each of their orders for drinks. He quickly returned, with their non-alcoholic beverages, and politely asked them if they were ready to order. Dr. Matzin said, "Yes, I believe we are." They placed their lunch orders, and Lynn excused herself to go to the restroom.

Dimitri observed Lynn leaving the table and immediately recognized it as an opportunity to claim his first victim. He stood-up from his barstool, took one step, dropped his umbrella, grabbed his chest, and fell flat on his face. He was dead before he hit the floor. A small stream of blood, from a post-mortem broken nose, trickled on the floor to the right-side of his head—a white iridescent fluffy down feather perched, unscathed, on top of the small pool of blood.

Lynn returned from the restroom, to the hustle and bustle that ensued. There was a general state of panic exhibited by the customers at the bar, and it quickly spread to the patrons in the adjoining dining area. The hotel's doctor arrived on the scene, made his assessment, and asked the

hostess to summon the hotel's manager. Jean-
Claude, the hotel's manager, arrived shortly after
he was summoned. He instantly noticed the man
lying on the floor, and immediately approached the
hotel's doctor for an explanation. The competent
physician said, "The man is dead from what appears
to be a heart attack." Jean-Claude used his cell
phone to call his assistant, and told him to
contact the coroner's office because a patron had
apparently succumbed to a heart attack in the
Lobby Lounge bar.

Dr. Matzin raised his right hand to summon
his party's waiter. Jacques instantly responded
and asked, "How can I help you?" Dr. Matzin said,
"Would you please ask the hotel's manager to come
to our table?" Jacques did not have to go very
far, because Jean-Claude was standing a short
distance away at the bar. He casually approached
his boss and said, "Excuse me sir, I hate to
bother you, but Dr. Matzin, who is seated with his
party over there, has asked to meet with you."
Jean-Claude said, "Thank you," and immediately
left to speak with him. He quickly approached Dr.
Matzin saying, "I am Jean-Claude, the Shangri-La's
manager. How can I be of assistance?" Dr. Matzin
replied, "In consideration of the current
situation at the bar, I am humbly requesting that
you relocate us to a private party facility, and
have our lunch-orders delivered there. We have

important business to discuss, and it is too
distracting here." Jean-Claude answered, "We are
in the midst of a rather rare predicament, and it
would be my pleasure to grant your request.
Please, follow me."

Meanwhile, back in Woodsville, Natasha was
boarding her red Mercedes SLK300 Roadster that was
parked in the NCSCR parking lot. She made a left
turn, out of the parking lot, onto East Baltimore
Street. One block later, she made another left
turn onto West Plum Road. She drove up a short
hill to the blinking light, and stop sign, at the
intersection with Route 176. Then, she activated
her left turn signal, and stopped. She looked to
her left and saw a large dump truck quickly
approaching the intersection in the southbound
lane. Then, she looked to her right, noticed that
the northbound lane was clear, and logically
decided to wait for the dump truck to pass.
However, as the speeding dump truck neared the
intersection, the driver apparently lost control
as the large vehicle inexplicably swerved to its
right and violently broadsided the driver's side
of Natasha's Mercedes. Natasha let out a fearful
scream and witnessed her own demise in slow
motion. The dump truck bulldozed what was left of
her car up a relatively steep embankment in the
front yard of a private residence, and came to
rest at the trunk of a large pine tree. Natasha's

flattened vehicle burst into flames and ignited the pine tree. A few seconds later, the dump truck exploded in a massive fireball. Shortly thereafter, the Woodsville Volunteer Fire Department arrived on the scene, and the firefighters quickly got the vehicle fires under control, because the fuel had burned rapidly. The large pine tree took a little longer, but they successfully extinguished it in time, and the private residence was spared. Afterwards, they had the difficult task of securing the victim's remains—so, they could be identified and released to their respective families. The coroner's office was contacted to collect the unrecognizable charred remains, and the State Police were called to the scene to determine the cause of the accident.

At the same time, back in Vancouver, a hotel maid was in room 1004 gathering Dimitri's belongings and neatly packing them in his suitcase. The coroner's assistant entered the room carrying the umbrella-weapon. He handed it to the maid, and told her to put it in the suitcase. She complied. He politely asked, Is everything packed?" She said, "Yes, sir." He folded the empty garment bag, put it in the suitcase and zipped it shut. Then, he pulled the handle up, thanked the maid, and rolled the suitcase to the elevator that led to the ground-floor service entrance, at the

rear of the hotel, where the coroner had parked
his van. When he arrived, the coroner was loading
Dimitri's tagged and bagged corpse into the back
of the van. The coroner's assistant placed the
suitcase beside the bagged corpse, closed the rear
doors, and took his place in the passenger seat.
The coroner started the van and drove off.

The Matzin-Masden party was eating
celebratory cake, drinking coffee, and taking care
of business. They had been relocated to a private
party facility on the hotel's 6th floor, where they
were surrounded by an astonishing array of floor
to ceiling windows that intentionally revealed a
spectacular view of the beautiful city.

Pierre LaChapelle, the Patent Attorney, spoke
first. "The Brain Research Centre legally owns the
rights to MHOS and the formula Dr. Matzin used to
test the lab rats, because Dr. Matzin is an
employee. I have completed a Canadian Patent
Application, to quickly establish a filing date,
which the Canadian Patent Office will issue within
thirty days of its receipt. After which, MHOS will
be granted a "patent pending" status, and because
of the TRIPS Agreement, a formal announcement
could legally be released without compromising the
pending patent." Joe politely asked, "Please
excuse me sir, but, What's a TRIPS Agreement?" Mr.
LaChapelle replied, "TRIPS is an acronym for Trade
Related Intellectual Property Rights, and patented

pharmaceuticals are classified as intellectual property. The TRIPS Agreement set the 20 year minimum standard in the field of intellectual property that all 153 WTO Member countries have to respect, which means that we do not have to submit a PCT Patent Application." Joe curiously asked, "What do WTO and PCT mean?" Mr. LaChapelle answered, "WTO stands for World Trade Organization, in which the United States, Canada, and another 151 countries are members. PCT is an acronym for Patent Cooperation Treaty, which, prior to the Trips Agreement, required that their patent application had to be submitted before an announcement could be made. Time is of the essence, with a discovery as big as this, and I am doing everything in my power to expedite the process. Unfortunately, the Canadian Patent Application has an 18 month public inspection period, and a two to three year examination process before an official priority date is established. However, in our favor, the 20 year Trips Agreement commences with the priority date, and, as I have previously mentioned, the discovery would be fully protected by its "patent pending" status. The UBC Board of Directors unanimously agreed to pay all the fees associated with obtaining the patent and share any subsequently generated monetary gains with Dr. Matzin and Jimmy. In a concerted effort to be fair, they mutually agreed to a 20/40/40 split. Twenty percent to the Brain Research Centre, forty percent to Dr. Matzin, and forty percent to Jimmy. I have, in my possession, a contract that only requires your signatures to be made legally binding. I will also need each of you to sign the Canadian Patent Application, because the two of you are duly listed as the co-discoverers. I will submit the application on Monday, and I am confident that they will grant us a filing date ASAP. I sincerely doubt that it will take the full thirty days." Joe replied, "That is more than fair, and I am certain that Jimmy will be happy to sign. However, I would like to recommend a new name for MHOS. The drug apparently makes detrimental B-amyloid plaques soluble—therefore, I am proposing that we name it *Solutio,* which is Latin for soluble." Dr. Matzin said, "That is an excellent proposal." Mr. LaChapelle replied, "I was just about to bring that up, because the patent application asks for a marketable name for the product. If there are no objections, then it shall be *Solutio.*" Everyone agreed, and Mr. LaChapelle penned the name *Solutio* in the corresponding box on the application. Dr. Matzin and Jimmy very willingly signed the contract and application.

Then it was the Public Relations Director's turn to speak. Michelle Felize gave a sheet of paper to each person at the table and said, "This is a draft copy of the press release I am proposing to give to the media immediately after a filing date is established. Please take some time to read it, and share any comments or suggestions."

PROBABLE CURE FOR ALZHEIMER'S DISCOVERED

The Brain Research Centre in Vancouver, British Columbia has discovered a probable cure for Alzheimer's Disease. Their Public Relations Director, Michelle Felize, is crediting the work of Russian scientist Dr. Yuri Matzin with the discovery. On December 10, Dr. Matzin received an email from Joe Masden, an American, who believed that his son, Jimmy, had mysteriously written the formula for a chemical cocktail that would cure Alzheimer's. The formula included what was, at the time, an unknown chemical compound. Dr. Matzin quickly synthesized the unknown compound, calibrated the formula, and tested it on Alzheimer inflicted lab rats with some astonishing results. Each lab rat was completely cured without any detectable side effects. Dr. Matzin is currently calibrating the formula to test inflicted primates with some very hopeful expectations. At the present time, the Brain Research Centre is predicting that it will be at least two years before the drug will be ready to test on humans.

Ms. Felize gave each of them ample time to read the proposed article and congenially asked, Well, what do you think?" Mr. LaChapelle broke the silence, "Ms. Felize, your article is very well written and I believe that it is good to go." Dr. Matzin said, "Well done. I agree with Pierre." Joe Masden simply stated, "It's unanimous." Nevertheless, Ms. Felize would still have to patiently wait, up to thirty days, for a filing date to be established before she could legally release it to the media.

The chaotic business luncheon ended, as it started, with everyone shaking hands. Dr. Matzin told Joe, "I will continue to email you with any updates." Joe replied, "I believe that it would be best if you emailed Jimmy, as well. After all, he's a much bigger player in all of this than I am." Dr. Matzin nodded his head in agreement and said, "I will need his email address." Joe wrote Jimmy's email address on a piece of paper, handed it to Dr. Matzin and said, "Until we meet again." Dr. Matzin replied, "Thank you, I am already anxiously anticipating that day."

Back in Woodsville, the coroner was carefully removing what was left of Natasha, when he noticed a white iridescent fluffy down feather perched, unscathed, on her severely burnt sternum. He nonchalantly removed the mysteriously pristine feather and tossed it aside. Then, he tagged and bagged what remained of both corpses, loaded them into his van, and took off. The State Police remained on the scene attempting to determine the cause of the accident. They knew that the driver of the dump truck was at fault, but they could not come up with a plausible reason. They logically decided to wait for the coroner to ID the driver, after which they would investigate his medical history.

The coroner quickly managed to identify the driver, but the skeletal remains and medical history revealed nothing useful. Nevertheless, that did not rule out the possibility of a heart attack, stroke, or even an aneurysm. Therefore, the State Police listed the cause of the accident as "unknown," which effectively eliminated the possibility for any lawsuits. Natasha's body was preliminarily identified using her license plate, and positively identified by her dental records. The State Police contacted her employer—Dr. Rostov. Dr. Rostov phoned Natasha's father with the grave news, and told him that he would make arrangements to have her remains flown to Moscow. Ivan said, "Thank you, but I don't understand. Why are you calling, and making arrangements, when Dimitri is there?" Dr. Rostov replied, "To the best of my knowledge, Dimitri is not here." Ivan asked, "Then, where is he?" Dr. Rostov simply answered, "Not here." Ivan remarked,

"I am very confused. Please, let me know when to expect Natasha's arrival. I will reimburse you for any expenses." Dr. Rostov replied, "I will use tax-deductible company funds to ship Natasha's remains, and I will call you tomorrow with the date and expected time of arrival." Ivan answered, "Thank you very much, but I am getting worried about Dimitri's whereabouts. He told me that he was going to visit Natasha." Dr. Rostov said, "I don't know why Dimitri mislead you, but we should believe that he must have had a good reason. You will be in my thoughts and prayers, and I am very confident that you will eventually unravel this obvious dilemma. Take care of yourself, my comrade, and please keep in touch."

The coroner in Vancouver listed Dimitri's cause of death as a "massive coronary," and the Ident Officer successfully used Interpol's, very reliable, Integrated Automated Fingerprint Identification System (IAFIS) to make a positive ID. The vast majority of former KGB agents were fingerprinted and the data was stored in Interpol's IAFIS, in the early 1990's, shortly after the collapse of the Soviet Union. The digital data revealed that Dimitri Karloff lived with his father, Ivan Karloff, in Moscow. The Ident Officer phoned Dimitri's father, gave him the bad news, and informed him that he would have to forward the money, in advance, before he could ship his son's body to Moscow.

Needless to say, Ivan was in a state of shock. Dimitri told him that he was going to visit Natasha, whose untimely death he had just been informed of—less than one hour ago. Now, he was being told that Dimitri was dead, thousands of miles away from Woodsville—in Vancouver, Canada. He calmly asked the Ident Officer, "Are you sure he's my son?" The Ident Officer said, "His fingerprints registered a positive match on Interpol's IAFIS, and you are listed as his father." Ivan forlornly asked, "How much will it cost?" The Ident Officer gave him a very reasonable price, and suggested that he use a credit card to expedite the process. Ivan agreed to the cost, and said, "I do not have any credit cards, because I always use cash. I will wire the money tomorrow."

Natasha's remains flew out of Dulles Airport, on Tuesday, January 29. On the very same day, Vancouver's coroner put Dimitri's body, and his belongings, on a plane to Moscow. Both planes almost simultaneously landed at Moscow's Sheremetyevo International Airport, where Ivan and the funeral home's director were anxiously awaiting their arrival. The funeral home's director gave Dimitri's suitcase to Ivan, and transported both bodies back to his funeral home to have each of them properly prepped, by his employees, for the following day's double funeral service and burial.

Ivan pulled Dimitri's suitcase into his house, left it in the living room, and went straight to the kitchen to pour himself a neat glass of Tovaritch vodka. He took a small sip of the half-filled glass and carried it with him back to the living room. He took another small sip and set the glass, on a coaster, on the coffee table. Then, he nervously unzipped his deceased son's suitcase. He removed the empty garment bag, and immediately recognized the umbrella-weapon that was nestled among the clothes. He carefully removed the umbrella and checked its chambers for any lethal pellets. The chambers were full, and he instantly realized that the weapon was not used. His level of curiosity almost peaked to a point of no return. He placed the umbrella back in the suitcase, quickly downed what was left of his half-glass of vodka, and decided to ignore it. He was oblivious to his infamous son's intentions, and reasonably realized that, because he was dead, there was virtually no way to even make an inference that might remotely lead to a logical conclusion. He went back to the kitchen, poured himself another half-glass of vodka, downed it, and retired for the evening.

The next morning, he dragged his semi-hung-over body out of bed, stumbled into the kitchen, and made a pot of coffee. Then, he shaved, took a shower, and got dressed in his best solid black suit, with a white shirt and black tie, for his fully grown children's double funeral. He drank a cup of coffee, put the empty cup in the kitchen sink, and walked through the living room to the front door. He was just about to leave, when he suddenly decided to put an end to his curiosity with the umbrella-weapon. He turned around, removed the umbrella from his son's suitcase, and brought it with him through the front door to his car. He placed the umbrella on the passenger seat, and drove alone to the funeral home.

Natasha's casket was closed, and Dimitri's was open. Very few people attended the service. The minister said a few kind words, after which it was time to load the caskets in their respective hearses for the procession. Ivan was standing in front of Dimitri's casket, to witness the closing, when he gently placed the umbrella-weapon beside his son. The funeral director closed the casket, and the evidence was carried to a hearse that would transport it, for all eternity, to its final resting place.

After the funeral, Ivan went home, changed into his pajamas, and opened a full bottle of Tovaritch vodka. He sat alone at his kitchen table, with constant tears in his eyes, and drank the vodka until he could barely stand. Then, he stumbled off to his bed to sleep it off. He peacefully passed away in his sleep, of natural causes, successfully eliminating any connection to the failed assassination attempt. A close friend found him in the mid-morning of the following day—a white iridescent fluffy down feather perched, unscathed, on the pillow beside his head.

CHAPTER 29: FATEFULLY FROM BRAZIL

On Monday, January 27, Mr. LaChapelle
submitted the Canadian Patent Application. Twenty-
one days later, on Monday, February 17, the filing
date for *Solutio* was legally established and
granted its "patent pending" status. On Tuesday,
February 18, Michelle Felize gave her press
release to the worldwide media.

Dr. Matzin was still waiting for his
inflicted primates to develop latter stages of the
disease, while the Brain Research Centre was being
bombarded with phone calls, telegrams, emails, and
snail-mails from millions of people all over the
world. Each of them offered to bring a loved one
with Alzheimer's to the Brain Research Centre as
test subjects. The UBC Board of Directors told
Michelle Felize to write a new press release,
which thanked the millions of people who
extraneously volunteered to be test subjects, and
emphatically stated that an on-line application
would be available in the near future. Ms. Felize
immediately complied, the number of requests
sharply declined, and the Board of Directors was
very pleased. However, a beautiful woman, lying on
a beach in Brazil, was about to be motivated to
turn their world upside-down.

Adelina Vieira, the Brazilian supermodel, who
single-handedly internationalized the Brazilian

butt was relaxing on a shaded lounge, on her private beach in Buzios, when her cell phone rang. The caller was Eduardo, her handsome husband of six years, with whom she bore their daughter Angelina, who was getting ready to celebrate her fifth birthday. She quickly answered her cell phone and said, "Hello honey." Eduardo replied, "I have some exciting news. The Brain Research Centre, in Vancouver, British Columbia, discovered a probable cure for Alzheimer's, and they have just announced that an on-line application for human test subjects will soon be available." The quick-witted Adelina simply stated, "That is exciting news. We will have to discuss it when you get home. I love you." Eduardo said, "Likewise," and ended the call. Adelina quickly headed in the direction of the steps that led to her cliffside villa overlooking her gorgeous beach.

As she was making her way there—her maternal grandfather's fulltime nursing staff was attending to his needs. Her seventy-eight year old grandfather, Francisco, was barely coping with the final stage of Alzheimer's, and his doctors had conservatively given him less than one year to live. Come hell or high water, Adelina was compelled to make him the Brain Research Centre's first human test subject, and she was concocting a plan as she climbed the steep steps.

She entered her palatial villa, took a shower, put her hair in a towel-turban, donned a white cotton bath robe, and used her cell phone to call her brother. Her brother Sergio, a licensed Private Investigator in Rio de Janeiro, purposely let his cell phone go to voice mail. She quickly said, "Please call me ASAP," and began climbing the wide Italian marble staircase to check on her beloved grandfather. She was less than half-way up the staircase when her cell phone rang. It was Sergio—returning her call. She answered, "Hello brother, I need to meet with you tonight. Something very important is happening, and I need your help." Sergio asked, "What is so important?" She replied, "I believe that a Brain Research Centre in Canada has found a cure for Alzheimer's, and I want you to help me get our grandfather treated." Sergio asked, "Why me?" She replied, "Because you are an experienced Private Investigator, and I know that your expertise will get me a face-to-face with the doctor who made the discovery." Sergio said, "I'll be there around eight," and ended the call. Adelina walked into her grandfather's room, gently kissed him on his forehead, and asked his nurse how he was doing. The nurse replied, "About the same." Adelina said, "That's about to change."

Sergio arrived, on time, at 8:00 PM. The butler opened the door, led him to the drawing

room and said, "Sir and madam will be here
directly. May I bring you something to drink?"
Sergio replied, "A single malt scotch." The butler
said, "Thank you, sir," and left. Eduardo and
Adelina walked into the room carrying classic
martinis with olives. Adelina greeted her brother,
"Thank you for coming on such short notice." Then,
she and her husband sat down on the couch situated
across from the chair Sergio had occupied. The
butler brought Sergio his drink. Sergio said,
"Thank you," and the butler left. Adelina
uncrossed her legs, moved forward in her seat and
said, "I want us to go to Vancouver, where you can
follow this Dr. Matzin, and help me find a time
when I can meet with him alone." Sergio downed his
drink and asked, "When do we leave?" She replied,
"Early on Monday the 24th; we will take my private
jet and I will book the Presidential Suite at the
Shangri-La, which has two separate bedrooms. You
should spend the night here, on Sunday, because I
want to leave very early on Monday." Sergio asked,
"What time do you have dinner on Sundays?" She
answered, "At 7:30, why do you ask?" He said,
"Because, I'll be here for dinner." Then, he shook
hands with Eduardo, shared a kiss on the cheek
with his sister, and saw himself out.

Adelina's private jet landed in Vancouver,
early in the afternoon, on Monday, the 24th of
February. She and her brother checked into the

Shangri-La, and a bell-hop escorted them, along
with their light luggage, to the Presidential
Suite. They immediately unpacked and settled in.
Sergio helped himself to a drink from the mini-bar
and joined his sister in the living-room to plan
their next move. They sat, next to each other, on
the couch facing the gas fireplace that the bellhop had turned on—just before he accepted his tip
and left. Adelina said, "I rented a car in your
name. You will need to go to valet parking and
pick it up. It's a black Cadillac GTS sedan with a
voice activated GPS navigation system." Then, she
took a picture out of her pocketbook, handed it to
him and said, "This is a photo of Dr. Matzin that
I printed off the internet. Go to the Brain
Research Centre and follow him. Notify me,
immediately, if he leads you to a public place,
such as a restaurant, where I can stumble into
him. I will wait here for your call, so keep in
touch." Sergio said, "I will keep you informed,"
and left. Adelina disrobed and took a shower.

A valet attendant drove the Cadillac to the
front of the hotel. He left the car running, with
the driver side door open. Sergio tipped him, got
in the car, and drove off. As he was driving, he
turned the navigation system on and said, "Brain
Research Centre." A highlighted map instantly
appeared on the screen, and something similar to a
female voice started giving him directions.

Adelina got out of the shower, towel-dried herself, donned a hotel bathrobe, and began applying her makeup. Sergio stopped at a liquor store, along the way, and bought a six-pack of Molson XXX. Then, he stopped at a McDonald's and used the drive-thru window to purchase a double quarter pounder with cheese.

Perfectly made-up, with her shoulder-length black hair brushed to her liking, Adelina put on a black laced bra with matching no-line bikini panties and black silk stockings. Then, she eye-candied herself with a dark blue-green button-down blouse that revealed just the right amount of cleavage, and aptly accentuated her bronze skin and hazel eyes. She tucked her shirt into a tight black pencil skirt, and slipped her feet into a pair of hand-made Italian black stiletto boots.

Sergio pulled into the parking lot at the Brain Research Centre. He parked in an open visitor spot that faced the front entrance. Then, he twisted the top off one his Molson's, took a swig, placed the bottle in the beverage holder, unwrapped his burger, took a big bite, and patiently waited. One finished burger, and four beers later—shortly after 5:00 PM—Dr. Matzin walked out of the front entrance and headed to the parking lot.

Dr. Matzin pressed the unlock button on his car key, opened the driver side door to his silver

Prius hybrid, started the car and drove off.
Sergio started his car and followed him. A few
blocks East of the Shangri-La Hotel, Dr. Matzin
made a right hand turn onto Denman Street and,
shortly thereafter, pulled into the parking lot of
the Raincity Grill. He parked his car and entered
the restaurant. Sergio pulled into a nearby
parking space, and phoned his sister. Adelina
answered, "It's about time." Sergio said, "He just
went into the Raincity Grill on Denman Street.
It's only a couple of blocks from where you are.
Take a cab and I'll wait here in the parking lot."

Adelina phoned the concierge, requested a
taxi, and asked him to reserve a table for two,
under the name Sergio Vieira, at the Raincity
Grill. Then, she donned her faux-fur knee-length
sable coat, grabbed her black leather Coach
handbag, and headed for the elevator. In the time
it took for her to step out of the elevator and
walk into the lobby—a running taxi cab was
patiently waiting for her under the canopy at the
hotel's entrance. She quickly entered the taxi,
put her dark Gucci sunglasses on, and said, "The
Raincity Grill on Denman Street." The driver
replied, "Yes ma'am," and drove off.

The taxi pulled up to the front entrance of
the Raincity Grill. Adelina paid the tab and said,
"Keep the change." She got out of the cab and

waited for Sergio to make his way there from the parking lot. Sergio held the restaurant's front door open for his sister, and followed her in. As they approached the seating hostess, Adelina whispered, "The reservation is in your name." The hostess asked, "Do you have a reservation?" Sergio replied, "Yes ma'am—Sergio Vieira." The hostess checked her list, secured two menus, and politely said, "Please, follow me."

As soon as they were seated, Adelina removed her sunglasses, and began scoping the room for Dr. Matzin. He was sitting alone, at the third table to her left, drinking a draft beer and looking at a menu. She said, "Let's go Sergio—I want you to break the ice, and let me take it from there." They approached Dr. Matzin and Sergio said, "Excuse me sir, I-uh-We don't want to bother you, but—May we join you?" Dr. Matzin took one look at Adelina, their eyes met, blood rushed to his groin, and he answered, "I don't see why not. Please, have a seat." Before they sat down, Sergio extended his hand and introduced himself, "I am Sergio Vieira." Dr. Matzin stood up, shook Sergio's hand, and replied, "Yuri Matzin, I am pleased to make your acquaintance. Who is your better half?" Sergio said, "This is my sister Adelina, and the pleasure is all mine."

Dr. Matzin futilely tried his best not to stare at Adelina. A waiter immediately approached the table and questioned Sergio, "Mr. Vieira, have you and your guest changed tables?" Sergio replied, "Yes, we have. Dr. Matzin kindly accepted my request for us to join him." The waiter said, "Very good, sir. May I bring each of you something to drink?" Sergio replied, "I'll have a Bloody Mary." The waiter turned towards Adelina, who requested, "A glass of your best Pinot Grigio." Dr. Matzin said, "I'm good, and I am just about ready to order." The waiter left saying, "I will return shortly, with your guests drinks, and take your orders."

Adelina quickly decided on an entree, put her menu down, and aptly interjected, "Dr. Matzin, I'm not going to beat around the bush. I am here because you may have discovered a cure for Alzheimer's, and I am very willing to do almost anything to have my terminally ill grandfather treated." Dr. Matzin replied, "You look familiar. Where are you from?" Adelina answered, "Belize, and my grandfather has less than one year to live." Dr. Matzin said, "I am very sorry to hear that, but the University of British Columbia owns the formula and that takes everything out of my hands." The waiter returned with their drinks and took their orders. Adelina said, "It has everything to do with your hands, because one of them will inject my grandfather with the promising cocktail. I need you to get me an ASAP meeting with the people who oversee the Brain Research Centre, and I promise you that I will more than make it worth their time." Dr. Matzin could see the love she had for her grandfather in her beautiful eyes, and calmly asked, "How do you intend to make it worth their while?" Adelina replied, "That's irrelevant. Do you want the opportunity to test the formula on a human?" He quickly answered, "Of course I do. However, the UBC Board of Directors is determined to strictly follow protocol in this matter, which stipulates that primates must successfully be tested prior to even considering the initiation of any testing on humans." The waiter arrived with their complementary soup de jour and salad, a mid-winter tradition, and politely asked, "Does anyone need a refill?" In unison, they all said, "Yes, please," and the waiter left. Adelina asked, "Can you get me a meeting with the Board of Directors?" Dr. Matzin replied, "I won't know until I ask, but I am afraid that they will only tell me that their protocol is written in stone." Adelina responded, "What would they say if you told them that I will donate the Canadian equivalent of one million American dollars, to the Brain Research Centre, just to meet with me?" Dr. Matzin queried, "Even if they say no?" Adelina smiled and said, "That's right." Dr. Matzin replied, "Well, first of all, the Brain Research Centre is actually part of the

University of British Columbia Hospital, and I believe that your odds might go from none to slim if you promise your donation to the hospital. Second of all, the Board of Directors runs the whole university, and your odds may slightly go up, if you pledge your donation to the university. Either way, you are still dealing with very poor odds." Adelina said, "I am willing to take my chances. Can you arrange the meeting, or not?" Dr. Matzin honestly replied, "I would have to speak with the director of the Brain Research Centre, who would have to take your offer to the UBC hospital's director. Then, he could approach the UBC Board of Directors, who would have the final say in the matter." Adelina reiterated, "As I said, I am willing to take my chances. Will you help me?" Dr. Matzin paused for a moment, finished his beer and answered, "Yes, I will. Are you a model?" Adelina coyly replied, "Dr. Matzin, it is difficult for me to believe that a world-class scientist, such as yourself, recognizes me. I am very flattered." The waiter brought their entrees and asked, "Does anyone need a refill?" Sergio answered, "Yes, we all do." They quietly consumed their dinners, with each of them commenting on how good it was, and declining dessert. The waiter handed the check to Dr. Matzin. Adelina said, "Yuri, I will pay for dinner if you leave the tip." Dr. Matzin simply said, "Gladly." Adelina gave her credit card to the waiter. Dr. Matzin and Adelina exchanged contact information, Adelina signed the credit card receipt, Dr. Matzin placed a generous tip on the table, and they parted ways.

Sergio drove Adelina back to the hotel, let the valet parking attendant park the car, and they went into the Lobby Lounge to have a drink. Sergio said, "Adelina, I think you did well." She replied, "Do you really think so? I hope we hear from Dr. Matzin this evening." They quietly finished their drinks. Sergio politely asked the bartender to have a bottle of Dom Perignon sent to the Presidential Suite, and they took the elevator up to their room.

Adelina went into her bedroom, where she slowly undressed and put on a conservative nightgown. Sergio took a seat on the couch in the living room, used the remote to turn the television on and started surfing through the channels. He settled on a show on the History Channel entitled "Ancient Alien Visitors". Adelina walked into the room and casually took a seat on the couch next to her brother. She asked, "What are you watching?" He said, "It's a repeat of a show on the History Channel about ancient aliens. I think this stuff is fascinating." There was a knock on the door, and a male voice exclaimed, "room service." Sergio got up and opened the door. The bellhop wheeled a cart carrying a bottle of

Dom Perignon on ice, two crystal champagne glasses, and a gold foil bag of Godiva chocolate covered strawberries into the room. Adelina remarked, "Chocolate covered strawberries—yum." Sergio tipped the bellhop, and said, "Thank you." The bellhop replied, "Thank you sir," and closed the door behind him as he left. Sergio slowly opened the bottle containing the prized bubbly liquid in a successful attempt to conserve every molecule of its valuable contents. He carefully poured two glasses, handed one to his sister and said, "To *Solutio*." They lightly tapped their glasses as Adelina reciprocated, "To *Solutio*." They each took a drink, and Sergio walked back to the couch to sit down and watch the show about ancient aliens. Adelina placed her glass on the cart, and opened the bag of chocolate covered strawberries. She put one in her mouth, chewed it, swallowed it, and washed it down with the rest of the champagne in her glass. She popped a second chocolate covered strawberry in her mouth, and began pouring herself a second glass of champagne. The phone rang and she rushed to answer it. She picked up the receiver and said, "Hello." The caller asked, "Is this Adelina?" She replied, "Yes, it is." The caller said, "Hello Adelina, this is Yuri. I am calling to tell you that the UBC Board of Directors has agreed to meet with you. Does tomorrow at 4:00 PM work for you?" She quickly said, "Absolutely, I'm elated. Where's the meeting place?" He replied, "In the Administration Building on the UBC's main campus. I will meet you on the front steps at 3:45—if that's alright with you." She said, "That would be great. I am very excited. Thank you so much." He said, "You are very welcome. You can park in any of the visitor spaces located in the parking lot directly in front of the building. Have a good night. I will see you tomorrow." She said, "With bells on," and ended the call. Then, she rushed to Sergio and informed him of the meeting. He stood up, hugged her, and said, "This calls for another glass of champagne." She whispered, "And, just one more chocolate covered strawberry."

CHAPTER 30: A NOBEL—WORTHY DISCOVERY

Sergio pulled the Cadillac into one of the visitor spaces of the parking lot in front of the UBC's administration building at exactly 3:45 PM. Dr. Matzin met them on the front steps and asked Adelina, "Are you ready for this?" She replied, "Can you not hear the bells?" He just smiled, and led them into a room located a short distance down the hallway from the main entrance. The five, all-male, members of the Board of Directors were seated, along with the all-male directors of the UBC hospital and Brain Research Centre, at one end of a large rectangular table with twelve chairs. The president of the Board of Directors, Jean-Claude Maltese, occupied the seat at the head of the table. Dr. Matzin introduced everybody, and the three of them sat at the opposite end of the table, with Adelina, the only female, taking the opposing head of table seat.

Mr. Maltese asked, "Ms. Vieira, how does giving us the equivalent of one million American dollars help you get your grandfather treated with a minimally-tested experimental drug?" Adelina replied, "I never said it would. I made the offer to get this meeting—and, apparently, it worked." Jean-Claude was irritated by her response and asked, "Are you saying that you do not intend to keep your end of the bargain?" Adelina immediately responded, "Absolutely not! My word is better than platinum." Several of the board members chuckled, and Jean-Claude said, "Please accept my apology for being so blunt. How can we help you?" Adelina quickly replied, "Apology accepted. Gentlemen, my beloved grandfather has less than one year to live, and it has become very painful for me to watch him keep slipping closer to death. I am fully aware that the drug has not yet been approved for use on humans, but I firmly believe that it is the only chance my grandfather has left. I am also aware, from the press release, that Dr. Matzin is preparing to test primates, and that it could take at least two years to get the drug approved for testing on humans." Adelina stood up and continued, "I believe that the two year wait has more to do with obtaining a patent than anything else. Therefore, if you will allow Dr. Matzin to test the formula on my grandfather, then I will add the Canadian equivalent of four million American dollars to my donation, and I will gladly pay for all treatment-related expenses." Adelina sat down and Jean-Claude said, "Ms. Vieira, you have obviously done your homework. I need the three of you to step into the hallway, for a few moments, while we deliberate." Adelina, Sergio, and Dr. Matzin quietly left the room. Less than ten minutes later, Jean-Claude opened the door and invited them back in. The three of them sat in the same seats, and they patiently waited for someone to speak. Jean-Claude walked to his seat at the head of the table, remained standing, and asked Dr. Matzin, "When will you be ready to begin testing the primates?" Dr. Matzin replied, "I will be testing primates, with early stages of the disease, on this coming Monday—the 2nd of March." Jean-Claude asked, "When do you expect to obtain some results?" He replied, "Based on what I observed with the lab rats, no more than 72 hours after the first injection." Jean-Claude queried, "What do you expect to happen?" Dr. Matzin stood up and said, "Mr. Maltese, my esteemed colleagues, and welcomed guests—there is no doubt in my mind that the formula will yield some astounding results. The primates will, in my professional opinion, be completely cured of the disease without any detectable side-effects. It is almost as if the formula was created by God. We humans have not developed a single drug that does not have some potential side-effects." Then, he sat down and said, "Jimmy Masden was, for some unknown reason, chosen by God to deliver a side-effect-free cure for Alzheimer's to the world." Jean-Claude appropriately asked, "Why do you believe that it is part of God's plan?" Dr. Masden replied, "I don't know. For the life of me, I simply do not know. I can somehow sense it, but I don't know why."

Jean-Claude said, "Ms. Vieira, based on Dr. Matzin's testimony, it is the opinion of this board that human testing is much closer than we had initially anticipated. Therefore, I am requesting that you go into the room next door, and use one of the computers to complete an on-line application. Then, you should return home, as soon as possible, to make arrangements to have your grandfather flown here and admitted into the Acute Care Unit of the UBC hospital. He will be admitted as Dr. Matzin's patient, who now has our blessings to take it from there." Adelina emotionally replied, "Thank you, and may God bless you." Jean-Claude said, "Ms. Vieira, you are very welcome. I am confident that everything is going turn out for the best."

Adelina's maternal grandfather, Francisco Valdez, was admitted into the Acute Care Unit of the UBC hospital on Monday, the 9th of March. Dr. Matzin had already gotten the results he expected from his tests on the primates with early stages of Alzheimer's. Each of them appeared to be completely cured, within 72 hours, without any detectable side-effects. He emailed his findings to Mr. Maltese, who responded, "Congratulations, that is excellent news. However, let us not forget about the possibility for some long-term side-

effects." Dr. Matzin replied, "Thank you. I do not
anticipate any long-term side-effects, because
there is no need to continue administering MHOS
after the B-amyloid plaques and oligomer clumps
are dissolved. I would, however, recommend that
the remaining part of the *Solutio* formula be taken
on a regular basis to maintain the healthy status
of neural cell membranes, and that portion of the
formula poses no risk for any side-effects." Mr.
Maltese responded, "I am beginning to feel like
you in some ways, because I can inexplicably sense
the divine intervention you alluded to in the
meeting with Ms. Vieira. However, from a business
standpoint, I believe that it would be
advantageous for us to consider applying for a
patent for the maintenance portion of the *Solutio*
formula." Dr. Matzin answered, "That does make a
lot of business sense, because the MHOS part of
the formula, based on my observations, will
probably only be needed for a relatively short
time." Mr. Maltese asked, "What name should we
give it?" Dr. Matzin quickly suggested, "*Solutio-
M*." Mr. Maltese replied, "Perfect, let's go with
it. Should I include Jimmy Masden as a co-
discoverer on the patent application for *Solutio-
M*?" Dr. Matzin replied, "Absolutely, I would never
have synthesized MHOS without him." Mr. Maltese
responded, "Dr. Matzin, you truly are a good man.

I will get in touch with Mr. LaChapelle ASAP and personally see to it."

Dr. Matzin examined Francisco shortly after he was admitted. He recorded his physical measurements; and ordered an MRI of his brain, a CT brain scan, blood samples, and a urine sample. Then, he went back to his lab to calibrate *Solutio's* formula based on Francisco's physical measurements.

The following morning, Dr. Matzin viewed the test results and basically observed what he expected to find. Francisco's brain was inundated with B-amyloid plaques and oligomer clumps, but his blood and urine samples uncharacteristically tested normal for a sedentary man of his age. He cautiously proceeded to Francisco's room to share the news with Sergio and Adelina, and inject him with his first dose of *Solutio*. He said, "Your grandfather is undeniably in the throes of the final stage of Alzheimer's and he probably has less than six months to live." Then, at exactly 8:34 AM on Thursday, March 12, he injected Francisco with his first dose of *Solutio*. After which, he turned to Adelina and said, "I will give him a second dose tomorrow, at around the same time, and I will have blood and urine samples taken later in the evening. I am hoping, with a significant degree of confidence, that there will be some soluble B-amyloid in his blood and urine at that time. Try to relax and be patient. I will be looking forward to seeing the two of you tomorrow." Adelina replied, "Sergio has to go back to Brazil tomorrow, but I will be here. Would you be so kind as to have dinner with us this evening? I will pay for dinner and leave the tip." Dr. Matzin said, "I would love to. Let's meet at the Lobby Lounge in your hotel at 7:00 PM." Along with a wink and a smile, Adelina seductively replied, "It's a date."

Dr. Matzin went back to his lab to begin testing primates with mid-stage Alzheimer's. He later enjoyed a pleasant dinner with Sergio and Adelina; after which, he went straight home to relax and get a good night's sleep. After dinner, Sergio and Adelina anxiously spent the evening in their hotel room. Sergio drank himself to sleep, on the couch, watching television. Adelina took a hot bath, followed her nightly beauty ritual, and tossed and turned herself to sleep.

Early the next morning, as the sun was rising, Adelina watched Sergio's plane take off. Then, she returned the rental car and took a cab to the hospital to check on her grandfather. She walked into her grandfather's ACU room, kissed him on the cheek, and said, "Good morning grandpa, I wish you could tell me how you're doing today." He uttered something unrecognizable, and Adelina

responded, "I'm doing fine—thank you for asking."
Dr. Matzin entered the room and said, "Good
morning Adelina. Did Sergio's plane take off on
time?" She replied, "Yes, it did." He said, "I am
here to give Francisco his second dose of
Solutio." She asked, "Dr. Matzin, do you really
believe it is going to work?" He asked, "Do you
believe in God?" She replied, "Very much so; I
pray to Him every day." He calmly said, "Then, you
have nothing to worry about. It is going to work."
He gave Francisco his second dose of *Solutio*, and
said, "We should begin getting some positive
results later this evening. One of his nurses will
take blood and urine samples, around 7:00 PM, and
I will check the results tomorrow morning. After I
view the results, I will return to give him his
third dose. You just have to be patient. Why don't
you get out of here and get to know Vancouver?"
She replied, "Dr. Matzin, I do not need to get to
know Vancouver. What I need is to get my
grandfather well enough to go home." He said,
"Very well then, I understand completely, and I
support your decision. Please, continue being
patient and know that I am very confident that you
will soon get your wish." Then, he left her to
tend to his primates.

The following morning, Dr. Matzin entered
Francisco's room and greeted Adelina with some

exciting news. He said, "Adelina, I believe it is
working. Your grandfather's blood and urine
samples both contained a significant amount of
soluble B-amyloid; which indicates that *Solutio* is
doing exactly what I expected it to do." He gave
Francisco his third dose and said, "If the amount
slightly increases tomorrow, as I suspect it will,
then we will be well on our way towards curing the
first human of one of the world's most dreaded
diseases." Tears welled-up in Adelina's beautiful
eyes, and she said, "Thank you. Maybe it has
something to do with the power of love. I do love
him with all my heart." Dr. Matzin replied,
"Adelina, I wish you were my granddaughter. One of
the nurses will take blood and urine samples later
this evening, and I believe that I will have some
more good news for you tomorrow—believe, Adelina,
believe."

The next morning's scenario was very similar,
with one exception. Francisco's blood and urine
samples contained much more soluble B-amyloid then
Dr. Matzin had anticipated. He walked into
Francisco's room, and observed Adelina quietly
sitting in a chair beside her grandfather's bed.
She had her eyes closed and her hands folded
together. He reasoned that she was praying and
quietly whispered, "Adelina, I have some more good
news." Adelina opened her eyes and said, "Dr.
Matzin, you startled me." He replied, "I am very

sorry, but I have some extremely exciting news to share with you. You're grandfather's blood and urine samples contained a much higher amount of soluble B-amyloid than I had initially expected. This means that he's healing faster than the primates I have been testing." Adelina said, "That is wonderful news. Maybe, God is answering my prayers." Dr. Matzin hesitated, and replied, "You could very well be right." However, in the back of his mind, he had his doubts. It wasn't because he doubted the existence of God or the power of prayer. He firmly believed that Jimmy Masden had miraculously been used by God, in a very special way, to bring the gift of a new life to millions of people and their families. The obvious questions he had were: "Why?"; "Why me?"; and "Why now?". He will never be able to answer those questions. He injected Francisco with his fourth dose of *Solutio*, told Adelina that he would see her tomorrow, and quietly left. Then, he walked straight to the nurses' station and ordered the blood and urine tests. He was very concerned about the elevated level of soluble B-amyloid in Francisco's blood, and he wanted to be certain that Francisco's kidneys were functioning at a level that could handle it. He conscientiously contacted the dialysis department and informed them of the possibility that they could be getting stat orders for dialysis the next morning.

At 8:00 AM, on Saturday, March 14, four years after Jimmy heard the words, "He's 100% healed;" Adelina walked into her grandfather's room and Dr. Matzin walked into the nurses' station to check on the results of the blood and urine tests he had ordered. They inexplicably revealed that Francisco's seventy-eight year old kidneys were functioning at an abnormally healthy level, and therefore, his body could easily manage the increased amount of soluble B-amyloid. He immediately got on the phone with the dialysis department to cancel the potential stat orders he had requested. In the meantime, an amazing development was taking place down the hall in Francisco's room.

When Adelina walked into her grandfather's private hospital room, a wide-eyed Francisco said, "Hello, Adelina—could you please tell me where I am, and why I am here?" Adelina stopped dead in her tracks and began to cry. Then, she rushed to her grandfather's side, gave him a hug, and kissed him on the forehead—some of her tears gently dripped on his face. She used her right hand to wipe the tears from his face and said, "Welcome back grandpa, you've been away for quite some time and I have truly missed you." Francisco replied, "Have you spoken with Enzo about that job I told you about?" Adelina said, "Grandpa, that was eight years ago. You have Alzheimer's, and you are in a hospital in Vancouver, British Columbia miraculously being cured." Francisco responded, "Eight years ago—How old am I?" Adelina paused for a moment, still trying to regain her composure, and said, "It's the middle of March, and you are seventy-eight years old." Francisco said, "I can't believe that it's March. The last thing I remember was celebrating your eighteenth birthday in August, which was around the time when I told you to speak with Enzo about getting a job." Adelina laughed out loud and said, "Grandpa, I hate to disappoint you, especially at a time like this, but Enzo was only interested in getting in my panties. I chose to pursue a very successful career in modeling instead, and I married Eduardo Ramón when I was twenty. We have a five-year-old daughter, Angelina, who is your first great-grandchild. You are going to have to excuse me for a moment, while I track down your doctor. I will be right back." As she was quickly walking out of the room, she stopped and said, "You are going to love Dr. Matzin."

A few moments later, Dr. Matzin and Adelina casually walked into Francisco's room. A female nurse was recording his vitals. Adelina said, "Grandpa, this is Dr. Matzin. He is the man who gave you the medicine that brought you back to me and our family." The nurse smiled and quietly left the room. Dr. Matzin asked Francisco a few standard questions and told him that he was going to have to run some tests before he could even think about releasing him. Francisco said, "I will do anything Adelina asks of me." Adelina said, "Grandpa, I want you to listen to Dr. Matzin and follow his advice." Francisco nodded in agreement, and Dr. Matzin quietly left the room.

Shortly thereafter, a nurse entered the room to obtain blood and urine samples. Adelina was trying to tell her grandfather about everything that had happened over the past eight years. The nurse secured the samples, and Francisco remained oblivious to Adelina's failed attempt to update him. He wisely said, after the nurse had left, "Adelina, you cannot simply update a blank mind. I cannot relate to anything you are trying to tell me other than the apparent fact that you're married and have given birth to my first great-granddaughter. Frankly, I cannot recall attending your wedding." Adelina replied, "Trust me grandpa, you were there. I am going to have to leave you for a little while, because I want to speak with Dr. Matzin about the problem you are having with your memory."

Adelina quickly located Dr. Matzin and briefly described the dilemma she was facing in regards to her grandfather's memory. Dr. Matzin told her, "That is to be expected. In the mid-to-late stages of Alzheimer's, the victim's brain cells are incapable of storing memory. You're grandfather appears to have regained his memory prior to the onset, and that is an excellent indication in favor of the effectiveness of *Solutio*. You should be nothing less than overjoyed." She said, "Yuri, I am. Thank you so much."

Less than one week later, on Friday, the 20th of March, Francisco's blood and urine samples contained no detectable soluble B-amyloid and Dr. Matzin logically started him on a once-daily regimen of *Solutio-M* in capsule form. Francisco's blood and urine were carefully monitored for soluble B-amyloid twice a week for the next two weeks. The test results were consistently negative. On Wednesday, the 8th of April, Dr. Matzin ordered a complete battery of tests—which included an MRI and a CT scan of Francisco's brain. Each of the tests proved, beyond any shadow of doubt, that Francisco was completely healed—and, miraculously or remarkably, there were no detectable side-effects. Confident that *Solutio-M* was a very safe and effective maintenance medication, Dr. Matzin discharged Francisco saying, "Adelina your grandfather is cured and you could take him home." Adelina gave him a hug, kissed him on the cheek, and asked, "How could I ever repay you?" He said, "Be very discreet, and

pretend to know nothing." She replied, "I give you
my word, and you can count on it." He said, "I am
going to give you a two-year supply of *Solutio-M*.
I am very confident that the *Solutio* formula will
be patented and FDA approved in the United States
by then, so you will probably be able to get it
over-the-counter at your local pharmacy in less
than one year from now. Your grandfather will have
to take one capsule of *Solutio-M*, once a day, for
the rest of his life. You are very beautiful,
inside and out, and I am going to miss you. Have a
safe flight home." Adelina blushed as she
sincerely replied, "Thank you, but you haven't
seen the last of me. I will be in the audience
when you give your acceptance speech for the Nobel
Prize."

Adelina flew home, with her grandfather, the
next morning. She never said a word to anybody,
outside of her immediate family, with the
exception of the two nurses who had cared for him
over the past eight years. She had also, very
wisely, sworn each of them to secrecy, and
intentionally kept both nurses on the payroll to
successfully ensure their loyalty. Francisco lived
to be ninety-nine years old, and he thoroughly
enjoyed every day of the twenty-one year extension
to his life, as if each one was his last. He
rarely experienced a single problem with his

memory, and he quietly passed-away in his sleep from old-age.

Dr. Matzin's results with the primates he was testing were deemed outstanding, and the Brain Research Centre formally began testing screened human patients less than one week later. Each of the tested patients responded to *Solutio* in exactly the same way as Francisco. Everyone of them appeared to be "cured" of Alzheimer's after four doses of the miraculous drug. Then, each of the patients was given a daily dose of *Solutio-M* for maintenance. Dr. Matzin kept his apparently cured test subjects on *Solutio-M*, for the next two months. After which, he requested a complete and thorough analysis of each of his patient's brains and kidneys—via MRI, CT Scan, blood tests, and urine tests. The test results incontrovertibly proved that the fortunately selected test subjects were cured of Alzheimer's, and he was ready to announce his findings.

Early in the morning, on Sunday, the 14th of June, Dr. Matzin phoned Mr. Maltese. He informed him of the amazing results he had unquestionably obtained from his tests on the human subjects. He jokingly apologized for giving him the good news on what was Flag Day in the United States, and said, "It is time to announce, to the world, that a legitimate cure for Alzheimer's has been discovered." Mr. Maltese said, "I am certain that you would not make such a claim if it were not true. I will contact Ms. Felize immediately and instruct her to write a press release, with confidence, that a cure for Alzheimer's has been discovered. After which, I will hold a Press Conference and publicly announce your findings to the worldwide media. You will, of course, need to be present. I am very certain that you should prepare yourself for the media frenzy that will undoubtedly follow the disclosure." Dr. Matzin said, "I believe I could handle it, but what about Jimmy Masden? He cannot be left out of this. He gave me the formula for MHOS, and he gave me the recipes for *Solutio* and *Solutio-M*." Mr. Maltese said, "The public has already been made well-aware of that fact. Are you forgetting about the press release and the near-media-frenzy that resulted from it back in January?" Dr. Matzin replied, "No, I have not. However, I am concerned about making an announcement of this magnitude without including him." Mr. Maltese said, "Your concern is justly noted. I must commend you for being an upstanding individual, and wanting to give the credit where the credit may very well be due. I will personally contact Jimmy Masden and offer to fly him here in time for the announcement." Dr. Matzin asked, "What if he declines your offer?" There was a slight pause—then, Mr. Maltese said, "We will move forward, and it will be left up to you to personally give Jimmy the credit you believe he deserves when it is your turn to speak." Dr. Matzin said, "I can live with that—thank you."

Mr. Maltese immediately phoned the Masden household and asked to speak with Jimmy. Jimmy carefully listened to everything Mr. Maltese had to say and politely declined the offer. Mr. Maltese informed him of the magnitude of the situation and assured him that it was just the beginning. Jimmy ended the conversation saying, "I appreciate everything you and Dr. Matzin are doing, and I am truly honored that you want to include me, but I am very uncomfortable when it comes to being associated with a media circus. Please, give Dr. Matzin my best regards, and assure him that I will make myself available if a situation arises that necessitates my being there."

Approximately two years later, on the 17th of February, the Canadian patents for *Solutio* and *Solutio-M* were granted and issued to the Brain Research Centre in Vancouver. Less than one month later, the United States FDA unanimously approved the use of *Solutio* on Alzheimer's patients and simultaneously granted over-the-counter status to *Solutio-M*. In that same time period, more than 20 million Alzheimer's patients had already been cured worldwide, and they were comfortably living

their memory-filled lives taking over-the-counter
Solutio-M. Nearly one million wealthy Americans
were fortunately listed among them.
Unfortunately, more than 4 million U.S. citizens
still remained suffering with varying stages of
the dreaded disease, because each of the prominent
U.S. drug companies luxuriously wanted to obtain
the highest possible bid to mass-produce both
drugs. The United States government threatened
them with a bill that would grant tariff-free
status to foreign drug manufacturing companies
that had been mass-producing *Solutio* and *Solutio-M*
for the past two years. The U.S. drug
manufacturing companies were outraged, but their
greed-fueled quest, to put profits ahead of the
people, was replaced with significantly lower bids
that would make both drugs much more affordable. A
prominent U.S. drug manufacturing company was
quickly chosen; the multitude of angry American
citizens were appeased; the insurance companies
were elated; and the president will get elected
for another term. By summer's end, more than 4
million American lives were saved, and the world
was rid of Alzheimer's forever.

Early in the autumn, one-thousand very
qualified individuals invited by the Karolinska
Institutet to nominate candidates for the Nobel
Prize in either physiology or medicine,
unanimously nominated Jimmy and Dr. Matzin for the

Nobel Prize in Medicine. The selection committee by-passed the stringent formalities, and took less than one minute to jointly give the coveted prize to Jimmy Masden and Dr. Yuri Matzin. Then, they casually waited until the September submission date to make their recommendation to the Nobel Assembly at Karolinska Institutet, who also took less than one minute to approve the selection committee's recommendation. The award-winning revelation, naming James Masden and Dr. Yuri Matzin as the recipients of the Nobel Prize in Medicine, was proudly announced to the world on the 17th of October.

The awards ceremony was held on the 10th of December at the Stockholm Concert Hall, in Stockholm, Sweden, in front of more than a packed-house and the worldwide media. Each of the 1,770 seats were occupied by anxious individuals awaiting the formal announcement for the award in medicine, and more than an additional 500 people were standing. Rather coincidentally, Joe and Lynn were seated, adjacent to Adelina and Francisco, fairly close to the stage.

Apparently, saving the best for last, the Master of Ceremonies formally announced James Masden and Dr. Yuri Matzin as the recipients of the Nobel Prize in Medicine. Jimmy slowly stepped up to the microphone. The dose of valium, and the double-shot of bourbon, he had consumed at the hotel before leaving for the awards ceremony gave him the courage to speak.

In a relatively soft voice, he said, "Your Majesties, Your Highness, Members of the Nobel Assembly at Karolinska Institutet, Members of the Norwegian Nobel Committee, Your Excellencies, and citizens for worldwide peace: Thank you . . ." Francisco Valdez immediately stood up and rudely interrupted him in a loud voice exclaiming, "No! Thank you, Jimmy! I thank God for you!" The entire audience, nearly 2,300 people, instantly responded with a near-deafening, apparently never-ending, standing ovation of cheers and insistent loud clapping that seemed to last for an eternity. The King of Sweden stood on the stage, facing Jimmy, and kept clapping with the audience. The Master of Ceremonies stepped up to the microphone in a vain attempt to settle them down, but they just ignored him. Jimmy experienced a severe panic attack, and simply chose to re-take his seat on the stage. The out-of-control crowd eventually settled down and respectfully listened to Dr. Matzin honestly recount the entire story with integrity. Then, the King of Sweden gave Jimmy and Dr. Matzin their awards. After which, the audience erupted in a second, seemingly never-ending, boisterous standing ovation.

EPILOGUE: THE "PROMISE"

The Masdens chose to bypass the Nobel
Banquet, at Jimmy's request, and immediately flew
home after the ceremony. Shortly after their
arrival, Jimmy was inundated with an enormous
number of media requests for interviews with
magazines, radio talk shows, and television. He
firmly insisted on having nothing to do with any
of it, but his father tactfully talked him into
being interviewed by a well-known journalist for
Time magazine, and Matt Lauer on the Today Show.
Jimmy cautiously agreed to both, with the
stipulation that his parents accompany him. The
rest of the world-wide media would have to rely on
file photos, social media, and quotes from the
only two interviews he was willing to grant.
However, the viewer ratings for the Today Show
interview were off the charts, and Matt Lauer
slyly used his expertise to make Jimmy feel very
proud of himself. After the show, Jimmy's self-
esteem was at an all time high and he told his
father that he wanted to do another television
interview. Joe gave his request a lot of thought,
and settled on recommending Oprah. The next
morning, over coffee, Joe said, "Jimmy, if I were
you, I would hands-down agree to being interviewed
by Oprah." Jimmy paused for a moment and replied,
"Let's set it up." An aging Oprah excitedly came

out of retirement to host the half-hour special.
The viewer ratings for the Oprah interview
slightly exceeded the Today Show ratings, and
Oprah cleverly managed to further boost Jimmy's
self-esteem. The offers kept pouring in, but Jimmy
had lost interest. He decided to get on with his
life, and focus on what captivated him most—
Marlania, his family, his job, and playing guitar.

Jimmy was head over heels in love with
Marlania, and shortly after returning to work—he
humbly asked his boss to go out with him.
Marlania, having just recently broken-up with
her boyfriend of two years, was on the rebound.
Jimmy was her employee, but he was also an
available, very handsome, American hero. She
reasoned that there was no way she could deny his
sincere request, and immediately asked, "Where do
you want to take me?" He quickly responded,
"Dinner at the Red Horse and any movie of your
choice." She answered, "That would be great. When
do you want to go?" Jimmy said, "I was hoping this
Saturday, if you could find a way to make it
happen." She said, "Consider it done. What time
would you like to pick me up?" Jimmy answered,
"That depends on the movie you choose and the time
it is playing." She intuitively replied, "Make a
dinner reservation for 5:30 and pick me up at
five. After dinner, we'll go to The Promenade and

I'll choose a movie after we get there." Jimmy
said, "I will pick you up at five."

It was a match made in heaven. Their first
date went flawlessly well. Jimmy said all the
right things at the all the right times, and
Marlania's bedroom eyes pleasantly accentuated her
perpetual smile. She enticed Jimmy into kissing
her goodnight, and fell asleep dreaming about the
kiss she wishfully hoped to experience again and
again. Her wish came true. They dated every
weekend for the next six months, and Jimmy always
kissed her goodnight. She went to bed, every
night, longing for the next date and the next
goodnight kiss.

Occasionally, they went out of town to
Baltimore's Inner Harbor, Ocean City, and the
nostalgic rock concerts at the Verizon Center in
the District of Columbia. Jimmy was always the
perfect gentleman; because he was infatuated with
her, and quite fearful of doing anything that
might have a negative impact on their blossoming
relationship. Whenever they stayed in an out of
town hotel—Jimmy would kiss her goodnight, but he
never tried to take it any further.

Shortly after they started dating, Marlania
fell in love with him—not because of who he was to
the outside world—because of who he was on the
inside. There was a bitter-sweetness about him
that she found irresistible. He was well-mannered,

very handsome, and curiously shy in the presence
of strangers. Conversely, his personality was
dramatically different in the company of people
with whom he felt comfortable. Then, he was
outgoing, confident, and more than willing to
challenge anyone to compete with him. Fortunately,
his stressful worried side, directly related to
his life-experiences, miraculously dissipated in
her presence. He was not yet her lover, but she
mysteriously sensed a powerful, strong connection
on the day they met. There was no doubt in her
mind. She was sure that he was in love with her,
and she knew that she was in love with him.

On his birthday, Jimmy humbly asked the
beautiful Marlania to marry him as they dined at
Il Porto—their favorite Frederick restaurant.
After which, he "accidentally" dropped the
engagement ring in her glass of wine. She drank
the wine, retrieved the flawless two-carat diamond
ring set in platinum, and answered, "Yes." Jimmy
softly whispered, "I love you," and politely
asked, "Are you ready to set a date?" She
excitedly replied, "As a matter of fact, I am." A
relaxed Jimmy tenderly kissed her, on her soft
velvet lips, and calmly said, "I'm ready if you
are." She instantly responded, with the
unmistakable confidence of a woman in love, "Give
me a minute, and I'll give you a date."

Having lived in Frederick County all her life, Marlania knew from experience that the best time of year, weather-wise, was usually in the middle of autumn. She used the calendar on her cell phone to make the elementary calculation, and casually said, "I want to marry you on Saturday, the 4th of November." Jimmy replied, "I will be there, but you will have to tell me where "there" is going to be." She coyly answered, "In good time, my love, in good time."

Jimmy got home a little after midnight, and both of his parents were soundly sleeping. He quietly entered their bedroom and tenderly shook his mom until she awoke. She whispered, "Jimmy—what's wrong?" He whispered, "Nothing, I just have to tell you something, and I need a favor." She softly asked, "Can it wait until the morning?" He said, "No, we need to talk now." She yawned and said, "OK, I'll meet you in the kitchen."

Jimmy went into the kitchen, poured himself a glass of water, and took a seat at the kitchen table. Lynn got out of bed, used the bathroom, walked into the kitchen, took a seat at the kitchen table next to her son and asked, "How can I possibly help you this late at night?" Knowing that he currently had more than twenty million dollars in liquid assets, Jimmy said, "I'm getting married and I need you to help me find a small farm that I could buy, and I need it right away."

His mother asked, "What's the hurry?" He replied,
"It's a secret." She gave him a hug and said,
"Congratulations, I am so happy for you. When are
you getting married?" He said, "Marlania wants to
get married on November 4th, but I need to take
care of something that has been bothering me for a
long time, and I can't do it unless I purchase
some land as soon as possible." Saturday had
barely become Sunday, so Lynn answered, "You may
have to give me some time—but, I will do my best
to try and find something tomorrow."

On Monday, after Lynn got home from work, she
informed Jimmy of a 125-acre parcel of land that
was for sale on the outskirts of Emmitsburg, MD.
Jimmy said, "That sounds amazing. Please, make an
ASAP appointment with the realtor." After dinner,
Lynn phoned the real estate agent and made
arrangements to view the property on Tuesday at
7:00 PM. They met with the agent, and Jimmy
excitedly witnessed everything he wanted. The land
had multiple perked and approved home sites, and
incredible Catoctin Mountain views; which, along
with the geologically linked Bull Run Mountains,
comprised the easternmost ridge of the Blue Ridge
Mountains in central Maryland. However, when he
saw the golden statue of Mary staring at him from
atop the bell tower at the entrance to the Grotto,
located at nearby Mount Saint Mary's University,
he was sure that he was standing on the land he

wanted for himself and his family. He made a cash
offer of $725,000.00; and the owner—who wanted
$750,000.00—immediately accepted. The settlement
date was set for Friday, June 16.

The property was almost magically divided
into sections that perfectly suited Jimmy's plans.
There was a level 20-acre field that was perked
and approved for up to ten four-bedroom home
sites. He planned on building four homes on that
field—one for himself and his lovely wife-to-be,
one for his parents, one for Jenny and Bill, and
one for Jack. Each home would have one acre of
land for personal use; and one centrally-located
acre would be designated as the family vegetable
garden. The remaining 15-acres would be planted
with grapevines and fruit trees, and house a small
state-of-the-art winery that was capable of
producing an elite selection of wines. There was a
rolling 60-acre pasture that was perfectly suited
for raising organic grass-fed grazing animals;
upon which he planned to raise a few thoroughbred
horses, some black angus cattle, and at least one
donkey. The somewhat extraneous 45-acres of creek-
crossed forested land, located on the northernmost
end of the property, could be used for hunting and
fishing. He envisioned a fishing pond, stocked
with pond-trout and largemouth bass, in the near
vicinity of the stable and barn that would be
erected at one edge of the pasture. As an

afterthought, he was pondering the possibility of raising some hens for fresh eggs, and a couple of Jersey cows for fresh milk and cream.

After he finished daydreaming, Jimmy used his cell phone to contact Bill—because he needed a big favor. Bill answered and Jimmy asked, "Could you get a crew together to build a scaled-down replica of the stage that was used at Woodstock in 1969?" Bill replied, "I'm sure I could. How soon do you need it?" Jimmy answered, "By the end of next week. I need everything in place for a 4th of July surprise, and you're invited." Bill said, "In that case, consider it done." Jimmy replied, "Thank you very much. If you could pick me up tomorrow at eight in the morning, I can show you where I would like to have it built." Bill said, "I'll see you tomorrow."

Early the next morning, Jimmy was sitting on the front steps of his parents' house patiently waiting for his brother-in-law. Bill drove his white Ford 4x4 pickup into the driveway at exactly 8:00 AM. Jimmy got into the pickup truck and said, "Good morning—take route 15 to Emmitsburg." Less than half an hour later, they drove onto Jimmy's newly purchased property. Bill was very impressed with the location and asked, "How did you find this place?" Jimmy quickly answered, "My mom found it. Let me show you where I'd like to have the stage built, because I have to get back as soon as possible. I feel like I have more than a million things to do." Bill said, "OK then, let's get going." As they walked to the field, Jimmy was silently making more plans. He started thinking about taking one acre from the potential vineyard and turning it into a recreational area. He knew that he wanted the stage erected there, but he began contemplating a tennis court, a basketball court, a swimming pool with an outdoor Jacuzzi, a putt-putt course, horseshoes, and a picnic pavilion—complete with a large pavestone patio, outdoor kitchen, and fireplace. There would also be enough space for a large bath house—with an exercise room, an indoor Jacuzzi, a sauna, and a home theatre. As they were approaching the field, Jimmy said, "I'd like to have the stage built here, with the mountain view behind it." Bill replied, "You couldn't have picked a better spot. This is perfect. I can have it built, and ready to use, in less than two days." Jimmy said, "I am very fortunate to have you as a brother-in-law. Thank you very much." Bill said, "You're very welcome—but, we do have to get going, because I can't wait to get started."

Bill dropped Jimmy off at his parents' house and went to get the materials he needed to build the stage. Jimmy got in his car and drove to the local music store. Fortunately, one of the owners was there. Jimmy excitedly asked, "Could you

install a modern version of the sound system that
was used at Woodstock on a stage that I'm having
built near Emmitsburg?" The owner curiously asked,
"How soon do you need it?" Jimmy anxiously
replied, "No later than the 1st of July." The owner
responded, "Yes, I can." Jimmy asked, "Do you have
an employee that I could hire to operate the sound
system for one song, after it gets dark, on the 4th
of July?" The owner said, "I have several. How
much are you willing to pay?" Jimmy answered,
"Three hundred dollars." The owner replied, "For
that much, they will probably have to draw straws.
When would they need to be there?" Jimmy replied,
"Around the time it gets dark—somewhere between
9:00 and 9:30—but, they would be more than welcome
to arrive around five and have dinner with us."
The owner smiled, shook hands with Jimmy, and
said, "Consider it done."

Jimmy walked into the music store's parking
lot and called Bill on his cell phone. Bill
answered, "What's up? I'm at Lowes getting the
lumber for the stage." Jimmy asked, "Do you know
anybody who could dig a well and install a septic
system within our time frame?" Bill replied, "As a
matter of fact, I do—and, he owes me a favor. I
will get in touch with him, and talk him into
taking care of it well before you'll need it."
Jimmy said, "I don't know how to thank you." Bill
said, "Just surprise me on the 4th of July." Then,

Jimmy drove to a local RV sales lot and rented four of their biggest RVs for the month of July. After which, he made a stop at Allegheny Power to get the power line installed. The manager assured him, after Jimmy slipped him a hundred dollar bill, "The line will be in place, and activated, no later than the 1ˢᵗ of July." Jimmy, once again, contacted Bill and asked him if he could get someone to install electrical outlets for the stage lights, four large RVs, and some outdoor lighting. Bill laughed and said, "I was actually wondering when you were going to get around to asking me that. I've got that covered with another good friend of mine, and I am certain that he will have it ready to go before the 1ˢᵗ of July. Can you think of anything else?" Jimmy answered, "Right now, I can't think of anything. I really appreciate your help." A moment later, Jimmy called him back and said, "I just thought of something else. Can you get a few picnic tables and a Weber Genesis Silver gas grill, with a filled propane tank, and take them up to the property?" Bill replied, "That sounds like a great idea. Are you going to bring the hot dogs and hamburgers?" Jimmy said, "No, I am going to hire a caterer for the 4ᵗʰ of July. The grill is for the rest of the month." Then, he contacted The Savory Spoon Catering Company—to hire them and select an "all you can eat" buffet menu. He quickly acquired their services, chose their most expensive menu, and left to meet with the person in charge of the Woodsville Volunteer Fire Company's Annual Carnival fireworks. The congenial elderly gentleman happily got him in-touch with the owner of the company he had hired for more than twenty years. The owner agreed to meet with Jimmy, on the following day, to make a deal for a fireworks display. The next morning, Jimmy met with the man and anxiously signed a contract to have a rather unique display of fireworks at his special 4th of July family celebration.

On Saturday, July 1st, Jimmy took a deep breath of successful relief. Everything was in place—as promised. The stage had the electrical outlets needed to power the lighting and sound system. Each of the RVs were completely hooked-up with everything they needed to function. The caterer and fireworks specialist had been prepped and prepaid. The only thing he had to worry about was the weather. The forecast was calling for a cold front to move through the area late Monday night, bringing with it a good chance for thunderstorms—but, several partly cloudy, warm, and dry weather days—including the 4th of July—were predicted to follow. He could only hope that they were right.

Jimmy couldn't bring himself to relax. He started thinking about the time between dinner and the fireworks, and he panicked, because there really wouldn't be anything to do other than sit around and enjoy the scenery. The first thing he thought of was hiring a band to occupy the time—so, he got in touch with the owner of the music store. Fortunately, after making a few phone calls, the music store owner called Jimmy back and told him that he found a fantastic band, who would be more than willing to do it for $500.00 an hour. Jimmy asked, "How many people are in the band?" The store owner replied, "There are four musicians, but I am certain that two of them will bring their wives and children—so, you should expect to have at least ten people." Jimmy said, "Tell them it's a deal. I will double their going rate for one hour, from seven to eight in the evening, and they can help themselves to the buffet when they get there to set-up." The store owner replied, "I will give them the good news and make all the arrangements." Jimmy said, "Thank you very much, but that means I may need another favor. The store owner asked, "What could that be?" Jimmy answered with a question, "Will I need your victorious straw-picker to operate the sound system for the band, or do they have someone?" The store owner said, "The band does not have anyone who could operate the sound system. How much more are you willing to pay?" Jimmy said, "An additional $300.00—I am trying to make the evening special for my parents, because it's their anniversary, and I want to make good on a promise." The store owner replied, in a very serious tone, "Jimmy, your parents voluntarily worked their butts off, over the years, to do everything they could to help the children in our community find the right path to follow. It pleases me to help you honor them. The victorious straw-picker is yours for the evening." Jimmy replied, "Thank you, I really appreciate it—but, I would be more appreciative if you and your wife can join us." The store owner said, "Thank you so much for asking. You can count on us being there." After mutually ending the successful conversation, Jimmy phoned the caterer and requested enough "all you could eat" food for twelve additional guests.

Jimmy and Marlania decided to spend some time on their new farm-to-be. They arrived late in the afternoon on Saturday, and commandeered the RV of their choice. They unpacked their bags and went in search of rocks to construct a site for a campfire. They built the campfire site and went looking for wood to burn. They located a good source of dry wood in the forested area on the northern edge of the property, and made several back and forth trips to stockpile enough firewood for a few days. After their first trip, Jimmy started a campfire. When they were finished, he fired-up their new grill—to cook some burgers for

dinner. While the grill was warming-up, Jimmy took
two large Russet potatoes, buried them in the
ashes beneath the burning embers of his billowing
campfire, and said, "They will be ready to eat in
about an hour. My father once told me that
campfire baked potatoes are a dessert-worthy
treat." Jimmy did not know that his father did
exactly the same thing, more than twenty-six years
ago, at the family campsite that was located a few
miles West of his present location, on the night
he was conceived. He popped-open a chilled bottle
of Martini and Rossi Asti Spumante, and slowly
poured two glasses. Then, he handed one to
Marlania and said, "To whatever you decide to name
this beautiful farm—and you." She replied, "Right
back at you." They touched glasses, she said,
"Salute," and each of them took a drink. Then she
said, "Hey, I just had a thought. Let's name our
farm "Solutio." After all, the money you're making
from it is going to pay for everything, and it has
the amazing potential to become the place where
our family members dissolve any unforeseen
differences." Jimmy paused to think about it for a
moment, and said, "I believe you may be onto
something, but the name "Solutio"—which is already
famous—could adversely attract some undesired
attention. What do you think about Maryview Farm
and Vineyard? When I first came up here, I decided
to purchase the property after I saw the golden

statue of Mary staring at me from atop the bell tower at the entrance to the Grotto, and her glowing presence should be all our family members need to squelch any unforeseen differences." She said, "I love it. Let's drink to it," and held out her glass. Jimmy re-filled their glasses. They tapped them together and simultaneously said, "To Maryview."

Later that night, they slept together in the same bed, and passionately made love for the first time. Afterwards, they cuddled and soundly fell asleep in each other's arms. The experience solidified the fact that they were sincerely in love with each other, and completely erased all latent memories of any past encounters.

The next morning, they awoke fairly early and decided to attend mass at Saint Anthony's Shrine in Emmitsburg. They arrived, just in time, for the beginning of the 9:30 AM service; and fell in love with the location, architectural beauty, and atmosphere. Afterwards, they discussed the possibility of having their wedding there, as they drove to The Carriage House Inn for the Sunday Brunch Buffet in JoAnn's Ballroom. Fortunately, they were seated upon their arrival. The hungry patrons pulling into the parking lot after them were placed on a growing waiting list. A pleasant waitress took their mutual orders for coffee, and orange juice, and told them to help themselves to the buffet. They carefully filled their plates, with an abundance of delicious offerings, and quickly returned to their table to indulge. Jimmy began chewing on a picture-perfect slice of bacon and asked, "Do you want to continue working at the nursing home? I know that I do." Marlania instantly replied, as she savored a bite of breakfast sausage, "If you want to continue working there, then I do. More than anything, I want to be wherever you are." Jimmy said, "The only problem we have, as I see it, is the fact that we are losing patients, left and right, because of Solutio." Marlania replied, "That is true—but, I sincerely believe that it will be temporary. Solutio is not the fountain of youth. There will always be plenty of elderly patients that will need us for a variety of other reasons, with the, thanks to you, exception of Alzheimer's." Jimmy said, "I think you may be right. The patients will probably be somewhat older, but they will be able to recognize the family members that come to visit. That notion makes me feel even more certain that I want to keep the job I love. My father is retired and my mother could quit her job, if I give them control of Maryview and pay them a decent salary. I could also easily afford to hire some experienced outside help. Jenny told me that I could expect to make at least three million a year, for the next twenty years, from the Solutio patents. What do you think?" She answered, "It sounds to me like you have a plan. Your talented brother-in-law, your sister, and your brother would all be living there—and, I'm sure that each of them would be more than willing to help run the farm for free. I think we should keep working at the nursing home for three to five years and use any spare time to help out and learn how to operate the farm and winery. After which, we should quit our jobs and help your parents run the farm on a full-time basis." Jimmy simply replied, "That's exactly why I fell in love with you. You're a dream come true." Feeling like she had to get the last word in, Marlania said, "Let's plan on it and do it—with all my heart—I love you Jimmy."

On Tuesday, the 4th of July, the family began converging on Maryview around 4:00 PM. Joe and Lynn were the first to arrive, and immediately began setting up residence in the RV with the sheet of paper labeled 'Mom and Dad' taped to the door. Jimmy and Marlania arrived, just a few moments later, and quickly entered the RV to offer their assistance. Joe said, "Thank you, but we are just about finished." A couple of minutes later, Jack drove his satin silver Acura ISX onto the scene. He and his latest girlfriend, Angela, who was hot enough to melt both polar icecaps, greeted everyone and carried their bags into Jimmy's RV.

Jimmy quickly joined them, to point them in the right direction. Joe, Lynn, and Marlania took a seat at one of the picnic tables and chatted the usual small-talk. Jimmy, Jack, and Angela joined them a short while later. Jimmy politely asked, "What can I get you guys to drink? You can either help yourselves to the quarter-keg of beer, or bottles of water and cans of soda on ice in the coolers. I also have a few bottles of wine on ice with the water and soda. Iced tea, lemonade, and coffee will be available when the caterer gets here." Each of them left the picnic table to select and obtain their choice of beverage. As they were returning, two caterer vans pulled onto the property. The catering staff swiftly went to work setting up the buffet. Then, the members of the band arrived, and started carrying their equipment to the stage. The sound system guru arrived next, and began unraveling all the cords he would need to control the state of the art sound system that had been installed. Fortunately, with everyone distracted, the undetected pyrotechnic expert drove his van behind the stage, and started setting up the fireworks display. After he finished, he unnoticeably blended in with the rest of the "strangers", and helped himself to the buffet. Jenny and Bill were the last to arrive. They quickly set their bags in their RV and joined the rest of the family for dinner.

Approximately one hour later, around 6:30 PM, everyone had finished eating and the catering staff was loading their vans. The family evenly split the leftovers, carried them into their respective RV's, and stored them in their refrigerators. Each of them, with the exception of Joe and Lynn, was thinking that the leftovers would be a great midnight snack. Joe and Lynn had not eaten after 8:00 PM for many years, and they were thinking more along the lines of breakfast, brunch, or lunch. By the time they all returned to the picnic tables, the caterer's vans were exiting the property and the band was warming-up. Jimmy had a huge smile on his face, as he observed the band, because he was envisioning himself being at Woodstock in 1969.

The band started playing their first set at 7:00 PM, and most of the family started polishing off the beer and wine. Joe and Lynn danced to the band's rendition of Clapton's "Wonderful Tonight," and a request for a special song came to Joe as he was dancing with the woman he fell in love with more than thirty-nine years ago. He wanted her to know in her heart that he was still in love with her. After the song was over, Joe excused himself to use the restroom. After which, he slipped a piece of paper, along with a twenty dollar bill, to the sound guru. The sound guru gladly accepted the money, and curiously read what Joe wrote on the piece of paper. Joe had written, "Please ask the band, between sets, to play the song "If" that was made popular by Bread back in the 70's." It was their song, when Joe and Lynn exchanged vows in Buena Vista, Virginia, on the 4th of July, and he wanted more than anything to have the opportunity to dance with his wife to the melody and lyrics of the special song they had chosen to revere as their own.

The band played a perfect rendition of Bread's "If," as their next to last song. Joe politely asked Lynn to dance with him immediately after the band's lead singer said, "We are dedicating this song to Joe and Lynn, who are celebrating their 39th wedding anniversary. I sincerely hope that they will invite us back to play it for them again on their fortieth." It was an extremely emotional dance for Lynn, as she literally soaked Joe's left shoulder with the persistent dripping of very happy tears. Joe could care less, because he was dancing with his soul mate—the love of his life. The band appropriately ended their gig with Zeppelin's "Rock and Roll," because it had been a long time since the Masden Family had been relaxed enough to rock-and-roll. Everyone helped the band load their equipment, and they departed, at 8:55 PM, with Jimmy's shallow assurance that they would be invited to do it again next year.

Everyone, except Jack, was a little tipsy from the beer and wine they consumed, but no one was anywhere near being drunk. Jack quit drinking alcoholic beverages almost six years ago, and he had not imbibed since. The four ladies were seated at a picnic table giddily laughing at anything and everything. Joe, Jack, and Bill tossed a Frisbee in the well-lit area near the stage. The stage lights and pole lights, that were installed by Bill's good friend, blanketed a very large area with more than enough ambient light to see clearly. Jimmy tossed a few logs on the campfire and discreetly followed the pyrotechnic expert, and sound guru, into his RV.

The pyrotechnic expert was the first to emerge from the RV. He quietly made his way in the direction of the stage, stopped to pick-up an errantly tossed Frisbee, and handed it to Jack—who had arrived at nearly the same time to retrieve it. Jack said, "Thank you," turned away from him and tossed it across the field to Bill. The pyrotechnic expert quickly walked around the stage and, out of sight—out of mind, disappeared into the darkness. The sound guru emerged next, and immediately made his way directly to the sound control center that was conveniently located about thirty yards away from center stage.

Jimmy walked out of his RV with the white Fender Stratocaster his parents gave him as a

Christmas present, many years ago, strapped over his shoulder. In his left hand, he was carrying the Digitech foot pedal his father had given him as an early birthday present more than ten years ago. His right hand was toting the cords he would need to connect his equipment to the sound system. Everyone saw him, stopped what they were doing, and curiously watched him step-up onto the stage. He plugged his equipment into the sound system, and played a few test notes on his guitar. Then, he incorporated the foot pedal with a few more test notes, and casually glanced at the sound guru—who instantly gave him a thumbs-up. Jimmy nodded his head in agreement, and reciprocated with a mutual thumbs-up.

Then, with confidence, Jimmy stepped up to the microphone and said, "It was near the end of January, around ten years ago, when my father talked me into taking a trial guitar lesson at the music store. He drove me to the music store to take the lesson, and he anxiously waited for my decision. My teacher taught me how to play the beginning of Jimi Hendrix's version of "The Star Spangled Banner," and I became hooked. As we were leaving, I promised him that I would be playing the Hendrix version of "The Star Spangled Banner" at Woodsville High School's homecoming football game in the fall. I never lived up to that promise, and I really don't regret it.

Nevertheless, now that I'm a man, who will soon be married to the most beautiful girl in the world, I want to make good on that promise. We are not at Woodsville High School's homecoming—we are at something much better than that. It's the 4th of July, our country's birthday, and my parent's 39th wedding anniversary. I am standing on a scaled replica of the stage that was used at Woodstock in 1969, when Hendrix introduced his unforgettable version of "The Star Spangled Banner" to the world, and we are gathered here together on the land that will soon become our new home. If there was a more destined time to make good on an old promise, then I would probably be totally at a loss for words. I can sincerely say that I have never been happier. Happy anniversary Mom and Dad. I love you, Marlania. Dad, this is for you."

Jimmy stepped away from the microphone and began playing his modified version of Hendrix's Star Spangled Banner. When he got to the blaring rockets and bursting bombs guitar rifts, the pyrotechnic expert ignited a perfectly timed round of fireworks. The resulting combination of music and fireworks inquisitively replicated what could very easily be referred to as the "Macy's Effect." Macy's in New York City has hosted an annual 4th of July fireworks display that was set-off from three to six separate barges floating on the Hudson River, and/or East River, which began on America's

200th anniversary in 1976. Their nom de plume was to play music that, for the most part, complemented the fireworks display. Jimmy's guitar rifts were in perfect sync with the fireworks, which absolutely amazed his unsuspecting family and the sound guru. After the rifts, Jimmy brought the song home with the impeccable accuracy that Hendrix would have unquestionably admired as being his own.

The small audience cheered, and made as much hooting, hollering, and whistling noise as they could. Lynn was still shedding the tears of joy that began with the fireworks display. Joe casually pulled a Bic lighter out of the right-side pocket of his khaki cargo shorts, held it over his head in his right hand, and lit it to request an encore. Jimmy, who had left the stage and was walking toward his parents, quickly turned around and stepped back up onto the stage. He immediately noticed a glistening white iridescent fluffy down feather on the stage where he had just been standing. He curiously picked the feather up, gently placed it in the left-side pocket of his jeans, stepped up to the microphone and said, "Thank you Dad, I really appreciate it—but, maybe later." Then, he stepped down from the stage, and once again began walking in the direction of his parents.

Joe turned to Lynn and tenderly used his thumbs to wipe the tears from her cheeks. He cheerfully hugged her and said, "Happy anniversary, sweetheart—I love you." She quietly whispered, in a very sexy voice, "I love you more," and passionately kissed him. Then, as if on cue, the pyrotechnic expert ignited a second very colorful round of breathtaking fireworks.

"Que sera, sera."

ABOUT THE AUTHOR

Robert Marcin was born in Westchester County, New York in 1954. He has a BS Ed. and an MA. He is a retired middle school science teacher, and this is his first book. He and his wife, Valerie, were married in 1977. They have three children, two grandchildren, and a small dog named "Rocky."